THE MICAH ROAD MYSTERIES
SHADOWS IN TENEBRAY FOREST

by Sara Lynne Hilton

Copyright © 2012 by Sara Lynne Hilton

Special thanks to editors: Amy White, Jan Boone, Gert Wolfert

Published by GEMS Girls' Clubs, a division of Dynamic Youth Ministries
Grand Rapids, MI

Visit us at: www.gemsgc.org

GEMS Girls' Clubs is an international, non-profit organization. For
the past fifty-four years we have been ministering to women and girls
around the world through club programs and other faith-based types of
outreach that demonstrate what it means to act justly, love mercy, and
walk humbly with God.

Requests for information should be addressed to: Micah Road Mysteries,
GEMS Girls' Clubs, PO Box 7259, Grand Rapids, MI 49510.

Educators and librarians, for a variety of helpful tools visit us at: www.gemsgc.org/mrm

This book is a work of fiction. Any similarities to real persons, living or dead, is coinci-
dental and not intended by the author.

ISBN 978-0-615-60182-3

Cover and interior illustrations by Elisa Chavarri
Layout and cover design by Tina DeKam

Printed in the United States of America

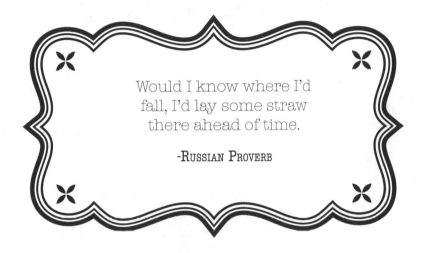

Would I know where I'd
fall, I'd lay some straw
there ahead of time.

-RUSSIAN PROVERB

In memory of my grandpa, Ralph Sytsma.
He gave me so much straw.

Table of Contents

....

CONFIDENTIAL

CASE FILE

CLIENT NAME
Filip Basara

CASE DESCRIPTION
Filip is accused of smashing a car and writing threatening messages on it. We agreed to take Filip's case, but we think he might be lying.

One

....

THE FALL

I felt like I was being watched, but the forest plays tricks on your mind. Like the way a loud rustle in the underbrush is nothing but a small squirrel, or how you are sure you see a bear but then it turns out to be nothing more than the shadow of a branch. After a while it's hard to know what is real in the forest. I ended up dismissing everything—even the things I should have been afraid of.

Now it was too late.

The branches cracked behind me, and I didn't have time to turn before I felt someone grab the back of my coat. The button on my coat dug into the center of my throat. I gagged and then slid backward through the thick, dried pine needles. Then I was down, sprawled on my back.

I started to cry. I didn't mean to cry, but I couldn't help it. It had all been too much. The tears streamed down my face and dripped into my ears. I realized one sharp pine needle had pierced the top of my thumb. I didn't even think to pull it out. I just looked up at the figure hovering over me and I had one thought: *You never know where you will fall.*

Two

LEAVE OR ELSE

Six days earlier…

Have you ever fallen off your bike and noticed that there's that second right before you hit the pavement when your body gets ready for the pain and your skin almost crawls? That's how I felt when Filip Basara walked into our office. It was like that split second before the pain.

Filip was sitting in our office because he was a criminal. Three days earlier, two girls were home alone when someone walked up the driveway, smashed a car, and spray painted the message, *Leave or else,* on the hood. There was also a

second strange message sprayed on the car: *TWG*. One of the girls saw the criminal's face. That criminal was Filip Basara, and now he was sitting in our office asking us for help.

My best friend, Tasha, and I own *The Micah Road Detective Agency*. Filip wasn't exactly the kind of client we were used to having. When we had the idea to open a detective agency we had all sorts of dreams about solving huge cases. We converted the playhouse in Tasha's backyard into our office and began looking for big mysteries to solve. But then our first two cases were finding lost cats and that kind of became our specialty. I don't want to complain. It was great to return a cat to a kid and see all that joy, but I guess when we had the idea of starting our agency I envisioned us doing really big things. But then the moment I had a chance to do something really big, I just wanted to go back to cats. I guess we always want what we don't have. And I guess when things actually happen they never feel exactly the way we expected them to feel.

Filip brought along his great-grandmother who had been with him when he was arrested. She was Polish and her name was Zocha. Zocha was tiny-boned, hunched, and spoke with an accent so thick and wonderful I wished I could soak it up and make it flow off my tongue for the rest of my life. I liked her immediately. I can't say the same for Filip.

"What can we do for you?" I asked Filip once we had all settled in.

"I didn't do it," he replied. And that was all he said. He just sat there and looked at us. An eyewitness had seen him commit the crime, he had been arrested, charges were pending, and all Filip Basara had to say was, "I didn't do it."

I just looked at him and thought, *Who does he think we are? Does he really think we can snap our fingers and fix this just because he claims he didn't do it?*

"Can you tell us what happened?" Tasha asked Filip, trying to get him to say more than *I didn't do it.*

"Didn't you see it on the news?" Filip asked.

We had seen it on the news. For the past three days this strange crime had been the lead story.

"Yes," Tasha replied, "But as detectives it is important for us to hear it from you, in your own words."

I nodded in agreement and thought about the part Tasha didn't say. It is important because we needed to get Filip to start talking. Once people start talking, clues slip out. Once people start talking they forget to hide the things they want to keep hidden.

"Go ahead," Zocha prodded. "Tell them what is wrong, Filip." She gave him a pat on his knee. I noticed the way her veins stuck out on her hands like blue bumpy mountains.

"This past Monday night two police officers showed up at our house and asked me where I had been," Filip began, "and when I didn't have an alibi, they said I had to come down to the station with an adult."

Zocha cut in, "I went with him."

"Where were your parents?" I asked.

It was Zocha who answered. "Filip's parents passed away when he was very young. I raise him."

"I'm so sorry," I said, embarrassed.

"It's okay," Filip answered. "You didn't know."

Tasha looked sympathetic and then asked, "What happened at the station?"

"They started asking me all sorts of questions about where I had been after school and if I knew Elsie Gowler and Maya Allsburg."

"What did you tell them?" Tasha asked.

"I told them Maya and Elsie are in my science class, but I don't really know them. We've never really talked or anything."

"Where were you Monday night?" My question was for Filip, but I was looking at Zocha, and it must have seemed like I was accusing her of something.

"I was home," Zocha answered with a gentle smile, "but you meant Filip, didn't you?"

I nodded, embarrassed again, and turned to Filip, "Where were you?" I asked.

"I was working on En-Gin-Unity Prize. One of my grandma's friends lets me use his garage and his tools. But he wasn't home on Monday."

The En-Gin-Unity Prize was a major competition put on by a local university. Every year they put out a different challenge. Students competed by using engineering skills to create a solution. This year the challenge was to find a way to provide clean water to people who don't have any. Apparently it isn't easy to dig and maintain clean wells in remote places that don't have electricity or good roads.

"My grandson is very brilliant," said Zocha. "I wish I could tell you his smart idea, but no, it is secret until the competition and until the judges see his brilliant mind."

The En-Gin-Unity Prize was a big deal. The winner received $3,000 in prize money and got the opportunity to work with a university professor to perfect their design.

"The police didn't believe anything I said," Filip continued. "They just kept asking me the same questions over and over and then finally said they had an eyewitness who saw me vandalize the car. So they charged me."

"Did anyone see you come or go from the garage?" I asked.

"No," he answered. "I was completely alone."

"Who is the eyewitness?" Tasha asked.

Filip looked down at his lap. "Maya said she saw me do it."

"He didn't do it," Zocha cut in. "Not my Filip."

Tasha nodded at Zocha before turning back to Filip. "Were you anywhere near the vandalized car at the time?"

"No." He was frustrated. "I was at the garage."

I'll be honest—I didn't believe anything Filip said. I was certain he was lying.

"What did they charge you with?" asked Tasha.

"It would have been just a minor vandalism charge, but whoever did it wrote the message on the car. They said it wasn't just vandalism. They said I was trying to threaten the girls, so they are charging me with the maximum penalty." He slid a piece of paper across the desk. "I met with the lawyer they assigned me. This is what I'm facing."

I stood over Tasha's shoulder and read the list.

1. **Repair costs for damaged property**
2. **Counseling for anger issues**
3. **Fines**
4. **Detention in a juvenile facility**

A juvenile detention facility? I thought. *That's like jail.* Why were Filip and Zocha here? The highlight of our career had been crawling under a porch to find a lost kitten. We were not qualified to help with this case.

"What did your lawyer say?" I asked.

"He said unless I could find someone who could vouch for where I was during the crime, I didn't have much of a case."

"Do you think you were set up?" I asked.

"I don't know," said Filip, "but I didn't do it."

"What about *TWG*?" I asked. "Does that mean anything to you?"

"No," he replied.

"Tell them about En-Gin-Unity," prodded Zocha.

Filip nodded and said, "Today, Principal Morely told me that she was disqualifying me from the competition. There is an integrity reference that she has to sign on my behalf. It states that I'm not the kind of person who would steal ideas or plans. She said she couldn't sign the paper with charges pending. I've worked on this for six months. The deadline is next Monday. If she doesn't sign it by then, I'm out of the competition." He looked up at Tasha, but avoided my eyes. "I think I had a really good shot at winning this year. I was going to use the money for my grandma. She hasn't been back to Poland since before I was born. She has a sister there that she hasn't seen in a very long time. We were going to visit Poland together if I won."

"Filip, it is okay," said Zocha. "It is just a trip. Someday we will find a way to go. We will go home again."

Filip just looked at the floor.

Tasha was so empathetic as Filip talked. I'll be honest, we have different approaches to people. We see people differently. She always sees the good in people and assumes they are innocent. She figures they wouldn't want us prying around if they were really guilty. I'm not as trusting. I always assume people have something to hide. Which I guess we all do, right? None of us would like the contents of our head poured out onto the table. There is always something in there that shouldn't be. I found it very hard to trust Filip. The police charged him and there was an eyewitness. It was really difficult for me to look at him and see anything other than guilt.

"You will help us, yes?" asked Zocha.

"Of course," responded Tasha.

Zocha looked at me and I nodded politely, but she didn't look away. Something in her gaze made me feel extremely uncomfortable. "You will help us, too?" she asked.

I nodded again and then blushed, which is weird because I'm not a blusher. "Yes," I finally said, "I will help."

"Thank you," she said. She looked back to Tasha. "What do you need from us?"

Tasha eyed me and then continued. "Did you get a copy of the police report?" she asked.

"We did." Filip handed a folder to Tasha.

"This will help," she said. "After you leave we'll head over to Elsie's house to look around, and tomorrow we'll talk to the principal and see if we can convince her to let you in the competition. We'll try to get some information and then contact you."

"Thank you, Tasha," said Zocha as she stood. She looked at me again, "Thank you, Chloe."

We walked them out and then returned to our office. Tasha sat at the desk and started reading the police report. She summarized as she read, "So Maya was at Elsie's house. Elsie's parents were gone. They heard noises outside. Maya went to the window and saw Filip spray painting the car and then saw him run into the forest. They called the police, but I guess Filip was gone by then. The car was smashed and spray painted with two messages, *Leave or else* and *TWG*."

"Why would Maya lie?" I wondered out loud. "I mean, she doesn't even really know Filip. I know she and Elsie have nothing to do with En-Gin-Unity. It doesn't make sense for her to just lie to hurt Filip."

"But," argued Tasha, "maybe you think that because you know Maya and Elsie better than Filip. I mean, we have to be fair and neutral. Why would Filip vandalize a car? What would be his motive? That doesn't make sense either."

I finally asked the question that had been bothering me the most. "Why us?"

Tasha shook her head, and I knew she understood what I was asking. Why did they want us to help them? We were two girls who found lost cats—little furry animals that like to cuddle and purr. We didn't handle the police, charges, threats, or juvenile detention. "I'm not sure," Tasha finally answered.

Despite our questions, we started packing our backpacks for the walk to Elsie's. Neither one of us had mentioned Tenebray, but we both knew we'd have to enter it. Elsie lived in the sprawling Tenebray National Forest. It was so expansive that every year hikers got lost and the police and locals would have to form large search parties to look for them. The tree cover was so dense that even on the sunniest day the forest was cool and dim and shadowy. And because of the thick cover, hikers were warned that the sun seemed to set an hour earlier in Tenebray Forest.

If we could have poured the contents of both of our heads on the table, we would have found a big globby pile of fear. It was like we both knew there was nothing safe about entering the dark and moving shadows that crept and hid among the giant trees of Tenebray.

"Ready?" Tasha asked once we were packed.

I nodded and, despite our fear, we began walking toward Tenebray Forest. Maybe that moment we started walking was the moment that changed everything—the moment of that free fall into something bigger than myself. Although I'm learning that you can never really find the beginning or the end of a big moment. It was like that second on the bike. I was already in the fall and there was nothing more to do but hope for as little hurt as possible.

Three

INTO THE FOREST

There are exactly three houses in Tenebray Forest, and I had never been to any of them. The houses in the forest aren't exactly places you just happen to pass. Sixty years ago, Tenebray was set aside as a National Forest. The families who owned houses on the land were allowed to stay. There were at least a dozen houses back then, but as time passed, most families abandoned their deep forest homes and their secluded lives.

As we walked, Tasha sketched a map of the houses so we would have our bearings before wandering into the woods. The three houses that remained were only accessible by a bumpy two-track road. About a half a mile into the forest, the two-track split in three directions. The center two-track led to the biggest house, which belonged to Elsie Gowler's family. The two-track to the left led to a modest cabin that belonged to Andrew Dodd's family, and the two-track to the right led to a cabin that was only used in the summer.

We knew Elsie from school, but we only knew of Andrew. Everyone knew of the Dodds. They were different; some people even thought they were crazy. I had heard once that Andrew's father was quiet, and if you happened to pass him in the forest he'd turn his head to the side as if he hadn't seen you. I heard that when people said hello to him he'd only give a half wave, which looked more like the way you'd shoo a fly than a hello. The rumor was that the Dodd's never left Tenebray Forest. They lived off the land, hunting and fishing for their food. Andrew was about sixteen, but he didn't go to school. People assumed he was stupid, but my dad once told me that Mrs. Dodd had been a teacher and taught Andrew at home.

"Why would Maya lie?" I wondered again as we walked toward Tenebray. "I mean, it just doesn't seem like something she'd do."

"Why would Filip vandalize a car? What would be in it for him?" Tasha wondered back.

"I don't know, maybe she did something to him at school or said something and he wanted revenge."

"Possible," said Tasha. "Or maybe it's the other way around. Maybe Maya is angry at Filip for something and wants to accuse him."

"Or maybe," I offered, "maybe Maya just thought she

saw Filip, but it was someone else." I said this as we reached the two-track that led into the forest. The opening disappeared into the trees and made me think of a train tunnel going into the side of a mountain. I thought of my mistaken identity theory, and it occurred to me that, if I was right, the real criminal was possibly wandering around Tenebray Forest. "Why would anyone want to live here?" I asked Tasha.

"Because not everyone is like you." Tasha smiled.

I smiled back. My parents have said that, even as a baby, I didn't like to be left alone.

We entered the forest. People always talk about the quiet of the forest—how they go there to get away—but the first thing I noticed was the noise. The singing birds, an upset squirrel chattering in a tree, the sound of a chipmunk running through the groundcover. When the wind blew, the sound of the moving trees made me think of the sound of waves. But the sound was overhead as if the world had been turned and the ocean was the sky above us. There was no silence here. The farther in we walked, the more I felt swallowed into the dark forest. Our feet made unnatural swishing and crunching noises over the pine needles. I was afraid our noise would attract a hungry mountain lion or a bear.

"How much farther?" I whispered as we came to the place where the two-track split into three directions.

"I think it's about a half mile more to her house." Tasha stopped and looked at her watch. "We're probably about halfway."

Then came the crack. It was a distinct snap that bounced

and echoed around the trees. "Tell me that was you," I whispered.

"I'm not moving," whispered Tasha. "How could that have been me? It came from over there." She pointed behind me. "Just beyond that big tree."

I looked to where she pointed. There was a giant tree shaped like a Y in front of us, and maybe fifteen feet past the tree I saw something move. But everything was moving. The trees were moving, the birds were moving, the squirrels were moving, the shadows were even moving. It was impossible to tell for sure if someone or something was standing just beyond our sight or if it was simply the forest playing games with us. I imagined all the things it might be: a bear, a mountain lion, or even a person.

"Something cracked that branch. We need to get out of here," whispered Tasha.

"Which way?" I asked.

Tasha was silent. She is the one who is always thinking things through, looking at all the pros and cons and making reasonable choices. But we were at the midway point — neither going back nor going forward seemed like the best idea. We just had to decide which way we were going and then go.

I looked back to where the noise had come from. There was something red, and even though I would later try to explain it away, there was no doubt about the other thing I saw: eyes. I saw a pair of eyes.

I grabbed Tasha's sleeve and pulled her deeper into the forest toward Elsie's house. I don't know why I chose that direction. I just knew we had to choose. As we ran I didn't have the guts to look behind us to see if the snapping sticks were simply the echoes of our own feet or if something—or someone—was chasing us.

Then, two things happened all at once. I saw Elsie's driveway, and I heard a voice. And because they happened at the exact same time, I felt a rush of something I never thought possible—two different emotions at the exact same time—relief at the sight of the house and total fear at the sound of the man's voice.

"You friends of Elsie's or Andrew's?" The voice came from behind us.

Tasha and I turned to see a man a few feet from us.

"Sorry," he said, "It gets a little spooky in there, doesn't it. I've run a few times myself."

"How do you know who we're looking for?" I asked accusingly.

"Well," the man rationalized, "not many kids come down this way. They are either looking for Andrew, whose road you already passed, or Elsie, my daughter."

"You're Elsie's dad?" I asked.

The man smiled, "I take it you are looking for her?"

We nodded and he walked out ahead of us and motioned for us to follow. "What got you so spooked?" he asked.

We told him about the cracking branch, but I had already been talking myself out of what I had seen, so I left out the part about the eyes. He led us to a large house set in a clearing. The house was a giant two-story with a covered, wrap-around porch. There were at least three porch swings hanging from various places. A large paved driveway curved from the garage, and it looked a bit odd to have the two-track bump into something so modern. All the Gowlers played basketball. It was obvious from the hoop at the side of the driveway that the pavement had been added as a playing surface.

Mr. Gowler led us up the pavement and stopped at the vandalized car. The bumper was dented, the front window smashed, and the spray painted words, *Leave or else,* looked more frightening in person.

Mr. Gowler watched our reaction to the car and then asked, "You heard about this?"

"It was on the news," answered Tasha.

"After your visit, I'll walk you back out to the main road. You two girls shouldn't be wandering around alone out here. Especially with this." He nodded toward the ruined car and then nodded to the porch. Elsie was rocking on a swing, watching us. We promised to let Mr. Gowler know when we were ready to leave and walked toward Elsie. She didn't get up to welcome us. Elsie and I weren't great friends or anything, but we had been in school together since third grade. We had done a few projects together. She was always so nice. So I was surprised by her reaction toward us.

"What are you doing here?" was all she said when we walked up to the porch.

"We're here for Filip," Tasha said. I love that about Tasha. She always has the guts to just be honest.

Elsie just stared at us.

"Filip asked us to help him with the vandalism charges," I added.

Not a word.

"He says he's innocent."

Silence. Elsie just sat there, not looking at us, not looking at anything really, just staring.

"Elsie?" asked Tasha. "You okay?"

She looked at Tasha for a bit and then quietly answered, "Yeah."

Tasha sat down in the swing next to Elsie and said, "Listen, I can imagine this is a bit scary—having someone come out here to your house and do this to your family. We are here because we promised we'd help Filip. He says he didn't do it. That doesn't mean we are against you, it just means we want to find the truth. If Filip did this, we want that truth. If he didn't, then we want to help find out who did."

Man—Tasha was good with people. I'll be honest—she's the smooth one.

"So can you think of anyone who would want you to leave this house?" I asked.

She shook her head.

"Can you think of a reason Filip would want to hurt your family?"

She shook her head again.

"Can you tell us what happened?" asked Tasha.

She shook her head a third time. "I don't want to talk about it," she said.

"We are just trying to help," prodded Tasha.

"No thank you," she said. It was an odd thing to say; it was like we offered her a brownie instead of help.

"Are you mad at us for something?" I asked.

Elsie inhaled, and for a second I thought she was going to cry, but then she swallowed it back. "Thank you for stopping by," she said as if she had rehearsed it in advance, "but I'm sure the police will do a thorough job."

I just looked at her. *A thorough job?* Who talks like that? Not Elsie. We were science lab partners for three whole weeks and she never said anything like that or even acted like that. I get that she was scared. I'd be scared living out here in the forest and then having someone paint scary things on my car, but *a thorough job?* Detectives have to be able to pick up on little changes, and this was definitely a change from how Elsie usually talked.

"Okay," Tasha said and stood up from the swing. She started walking down the steps, but I didn't follow her.

"What's wrong?" I asked Elsie. Tasha stopped and looked nervous. Elsie didn't say anything.

"What is going on?" I continued, frustrated.

"Thank you for coming," Elsie repeated, "but I'm sure…."

I cut her off. "Elsie!"

She looked at me for a second and then said, "I've got homework." She stood, went into the house, and shut the door behind her. I started to follow her, but Tasha grabbed my arm. "Come on," she said. "Let's leave her alone."

We found Elsie's dad in the garage and told him we were ready to leave. He seemed to be building some sort of bookcase. We waited while he put away his tools. He shut the garage door and then locked the smaller side door. "Can't leave things open anymore," he said as he locked up. When he turned from the closed garage door he walked straight into the vandalized car.

He grunted in pain. "I never park it up this far. Must have been in a hurry last time I parked it."

"Could the vandal have moved it?" I asked.

"Not without a key," he said. "The car has to be in neutral, and it won't shift out of park without a key in the ignition."

"Did he steal the keys?"

"Nope, got them right here in my pocket." He patted his pocket. "I probably just didn't remember."

We walked from the house back into the thick woods.

"Don't you get lonely living here?" I asked.

"Sometimes," said Mr. Gowler. "But lonely's not always a bad thing. It clears your thoughts."

"I think my thoughts got as clear as they want to be after that walk to your house," I said. "I'm all about lots of neighbors and no strange noises."

Mr. Gowler chuckled. "I understand. I used to feel that way too, but after a while loneliness turns into something different and you get a good look at yourself. You should try it sometime."

And for no explainable reason, a cold chill ran up my spine.

Four

NO JUSTICE FOR FILIP

"**G**irls, I'm not changing my mind on this."

"But it's not fair," I complained.

I'm not exactly sure what changed my mind about Filip. I'm not saying that I totally believed he was innocent, but after Elsie's odd reaction to us I just started feeling like maybe there was more to the story. And if that was true, I felt like Filip at least deserved to have a fair chance to work his way out of this mess. There was no way we were going to prove his innocence before the En-Gin-Unity deadline, so we had set up a meeting with Principal Morley to see if she could help us. But things were not going well.

"It's just not fair," I complained again.

Principal Morley sighed, and I could tell she was losing her patience. "Actually, it is fair, Chloe. Filip has criminal charges pending. I can't give my recommendation to someone like that."

"But that's exactly it," I argued, "The charges are pending. He hasn't been found guilty yet."

"And," she said with a note of frustration, "like I told you before, Filip may participate once the charges are dropped."

"But you know that's impossible!" I was almost yelling now. "It will be too late by then!"

Tasha put her hand on my shoulder to calm me. "Ms. Morely," she said in an unruffled voice, "isn't there something else you can do? Filip's first court date isn't until after the judging. Waiting just isn't an option for making this right."

"I understand, Tasha," she said, "I appreciate your passion for this, and we all hope this is a misunderstanding and that Filip is found innocent. But you need to understand what is at stake here. I have to stand behind his credibility, and I can't do that. This is his word against another student's word. I just don't know that he is innocent. And if I allow him to compete and he wins and is then found guilty, nobody wins. Another student, with the integrity the judges require, was denied the chance of winning. Do you see my problem? By allowing him to participate, I could be robbing another student of the chance of winning."

"But what if he's cleared?" I asked. "You keep saying, 'What if he's guilty,' but what if he's innocent? Then haven't you taken away his chance? He's worked so hard on this. That's not fair either."

"I understand your frustration, Chloe. No one is denying that would be a tragic end."

"Then can't we find a way to make sure that tragic end doesn't happen?" asked Tasha.

"Again, I understand your anger and frustration. I feel it too." I could tell that she was trying very hard to stay calm, but it was obvious we were slowly unraveling her. "I commend you both for your passion here," she continued. "You need to understand that sometimes justice is about doing what is best for the greater good and not the individual."

"But how is that justice?" I asked. "That isn't justice for Filip. Why can't we make it just for everyone?"

Ms. Morely stood and walked to our side of her desk. "Because life isn't always fair for everyone." She walked to her door and opened it, signaling that our meeting was over. "I'm sorry, girls," she said as she ushered us out the door. "If the charges are dropped, I'll be happy to recommend him." And with that, she closed the door and left us standing alone on the other side.

By this time most of the teachers and students had left for the day, and the stillness made the building feel as if it had lost its soul. Tasha and I silently walked through the empty halls. Ms. Morely had always liked us. I had really thought she would help us. I thought she would agree with us, and I really believed she was going to sign the form for Filip. I didn't know it at the time, but that was going to be the pattern with this case. Nothing was going to go the way we assumed it would go.

Five

....

IN OVER MY HEAD

After we left Principal Morely, Tasha and I slouched against the side of the school. We discussed whether or not we had reached the end of our investigation. We had been to Elsie's, we had talked to the principal, and we could easily rationalize that we had gone as far into the case as we were able to go.

"But is that right?" asked Tasha.

"I don't know," I answered. "I mean, how much do we have to do before we have the right to stop. Haven't we already done a lot?"

"I would say yes but... doesn't that just feel, I don't know, wrong?"

I didn't answer for a while. I knew she was right. I also knew that I had an essay due in the morning and the thought of going home, getting my homework done, and just hanging out for a while seemed more appealing than almost anything.

Tasha kept going, "We were going to be the kind of people who did things, remember? It feels like we should try to make this right."

I felt heavy. Getting up from my spot and diving back into the case felt as hard as getting out of bed on a dark, cold morning.

"Chloe?" Tasha asked after a long silence. "What do you think?"

"Let's keep going," I said, even though I really didn't believe in what I was saying. But whether I believed in it or not, I sensed that my decision to keep going would bring us closer to secrets that wanted to stay hidden.

We decided to split up to cover more ground. Filip had a meeting with his lawyer, and we decided that Tasha should go with him for moral support. I headed to Maya's house to question her about the night of the crime. When we parted ways we promised to meet at Filip's house around five o'clock.

Maya lived in town and it was an easy walk from school. The village of Tenebray is settled on flat prairie land that spreads out like an apron from the edge of the forest. Most of the homes are made up of farms and houses with lots of acreage. In the center is what we all refer to as town. It was basically a tiny, quaint street with a restaurant, ice cream shop, pharmacy, a small grocer, and a few knick-knack shops aimed at the tourists who visited the forest. It wasn't much, but it was enough.

Maya lived on a street just off the main road. Mrs. Allsburg opened the door and told me I could find Maya in her room.

I climbed the stairs to the second floor and watched Maya from her doorway for a few moments. Her ceiling sloped at either side so it was impossible to stand upright in most of her room. She was working at a small desk with her back to me. I knocked, which made her jump and let out a small yelp. She turned, looked at me, and scowled. "What are you doing here?" It was so hard to get a handle on what was happening. Maya and Elsie had always been so nice. Were they angry that we were helping Filip? I tried the same direct approach Tasha had used with Elsie. "We are here for…."

"I know why you are here," she snapped.

She must have noticed my body deflate under her harshness, because she immediately apologized and offered me a seat on her bed. I walked over and sat down. I had planned on doing standard detective questioning, but sitting on her bed in her room must have softened me. Despite her rude welcome, it felt more like hanging out with a friend than an investigation. That, and I was tired. I was tired of this case. I was tired of people being frustrated and short and rude with me. I was tired of being treated like I had done something wrong.

"What is going on?" I finally asked. "I don't understand, Maya. We went to see Elsie and she was about as pleasant as you just were. What did we do to make you so mad?"

Maya fidgeted with a paperclip. I studied her face and it occurred to me that she looked as tired as I felt. "It's just hard," she said.

"What's hard, Maya?" I asked.

"Well, I mean, seeing a crime is hard and then I guess having you and Tasha treat us like we are lying. That's hard."

"I get that," I answered. "But we never said you were lying. Filip came to us for help. He says he's innocent, so we are just looking for something that explains all this."

Maya's eyes met mine. "Listen Chloe, I know you are really into this whole detective thing, but you need to let real detectives handle this. This is a real case, with a real crime, with real detectives and police officers."

"I know that…."

"Filip is lying to you, and you are getting in way over your head. How do you think it feels for us? I mean, I thought we were friends, and it seems like you don't even care about how scary this was for us."

"That's not true, Maya. We do care. We told Elsie…."

"And how do think it feels to be out alone in the forest and then to walk out and see those threatening messages?"

"I thought you saw them from the window?" I asked.

"That's what I said."

"No, you just said, 'How do you think it feels to be out alone in the forest and then to walk out and see those threatening messages.'"

"I meant I walked out of the kitchen to the living room window, Chloe."

Mrs. Allsburg appeared in the doorway. "Is everything okay in here, girls?" she asked.

"Everything's fine," Maya said with a knife-like edge to her voice. "Chloe was just leaving."

I left Maya's house feeling angry and embarrassed and even a bit ashamed, although I wasn't really sure what reason I had to be ashamed.

Six

BREAKFAST WITH WOLVES

It was a few minutes before five when I knocked on Filip's door and several minutes before Zocha opened it. She welcomed me in and told me that Filip and Tasha weren't back from the lawyer.

"Should I come back later?" I asked, feeling awkward being alone with Zocha.

"Why no," she said. "Come and we will talk."

I followed her into the living room, trying to think of something to say, but nothing came. I was relieved when the phone rang and she excused herself. I wandered around the living room looking at different books and paintings, but it was the black and white photos on top of the piano that caught my interest. One picture showed a young girl with braids plaited on either side of her head. The girl was holding a chicken.

"That is Ania."

I jumped.

"I didn't mean to scare you," laughed Zocha. "I saw you looking at the picture. That is Ania the chicken. She was my first chicken. My father gave each of my siblings a chicken to raise when we turned six. It was to teach us responsibility." She said the last part in a low voice as if she were mimicking her father.

"Is that you?" I asked.

"It is," she answered. "And that was one of the most worthless chickens ever raised." She smiled at the picture and then at me. "My brother's chicken laid eggs like you wouldn't believe. But my chicken, Ania, didn't know she was a chicken. She followed me around more like a dog. Worst of all, Ania had this strange habit of pushing her eggs out of her nest. So every morning when I went to fetch the eggs, there would be a slimy, cracked egg on the floor. My father had never seen anything like it. He suggested that since Ania wasn't earning her keep with eggs, that she become Sunday dinner."

"You ate Ania?" I asked. I couldn't imagine eating something I had raised and named.

"Oh, heavens no," said Zocha. "I cried and begged and

pleaded with my father until I think he finally just figured it was easier to let me keep the silly bird. I could be very dramatic when I needed to be."

"What was it like in Poland?" I asked.

She didn't answer and her face looked as if she were far away. Finally, she looked at me and said, "It was fine at first. But then...."

I waited patiently for her to finish. I wanted to ask her what had happened, but I had the feeling I wasn't supposed to.

"My father took this picture minutes before he suggested we eat Ania," she continued. "It's strange now to look at the girl and the chicken in this photo. Ania had no idea that in just minutes someone would suggest she become dinner. And that happy girl," she pointed to herself in the photo, "she had no idea that in just minutes she'd be wailing to save a chicken."

Zocha fingered the photograph and then said, "There is a Russian saying that goes something like: would I know where I'd fall, I'd lay some straw there ahead of time."

"What does that mean?" I asked.

"I think it means if I could know ahead of time what parts of life would be hard, I would do something in advance to make it easier. Maybe put down something soft to land on." Zocha stared at the photo and seemed to be talking to herself more than to me. "But that isn't possible, is it? To know what will happen. And even if we did, I doubt we'd have enough straw."

Something hung in the air between us, like a fog that settles in and just sits above the ground. As Zocha talked, I felt like I was only on the edge of understanding her—it felt like what she was saying was very important if only I could fully get it.

"Would you like some hot chocolate?" Zocha asked.

I said yes, and she led me into the kitchen.

"Have you ever had real hot chocolate?"

"I think so," I said. "I drink the stuff from the blue box."

Zocha laughed and took out a saucepan. For the next twenty minutes she instructed me how to slowly warm the milk. We added cocoa, sugar, and a dash of vanilla before melting bars of bitter and white chocolate into the mix. From the fridge she took heavy cream and placed it in a glass jar and told me to shake it for a few minutes while she stirred the hot chocolate. She poured the chocolate mixture into two mugs and then instructed me to top the mugs off with the cream. She directed me to the table where we sat together. She lifted her mug in a toast. "To Filip."

"To Filip," I answered. I brought the creamy mixture to my lips. I don't know if I could explain that hot chocolate if I tried. It was so smooth and creamy and the chocolate was, well, it was like tasting chocolate for the first time. It was the best hot chocolate I have ever tasted. Zocha watched me drink and seemed genuinely delighted with my reaction.

"It is good?" she asked.

"I'll never drink from the blue box again," I answered.

She laughed, and I noticed that she had deep smile lines around her eyes that were completely hidden when she was serious. She took a sip. "This is good," she agreed. "You made very good hot chocolate, Chloe."

"I did have some help," I answered.

She set down her mug and watched me drink. We didn't speak, but the silence didn't feel awkward anymore—instead it felt warm. After a bit Zocha said, "You are discouraged, Chloe."

It's a very comforting thing to be understood. To have someone see something in you that you yourself haven't even put into words yet. That kind of understanding feels like a deep breath. "Very," I replied.

She nodded. "Chloe, there is always more than you first see."

"You mean we missed something?" I asked, hoping she'd give me the clue that would unlock the case.

"Perhaps, but, Chloe…." She paused and we sat face to face, looking at one another. I leaned forward, both afraid of the things she needed to say but also desperate to hear them.

The front door opened. Tasha and Filip walked in and Zocha's unfinished sentence fell with a thud to the floor. She held my cheek lovingly, like my mother used to do after I had a scary dream. Then she stood and embraced Filip before leading everyone to the kitchen table for some hot chocolate. I motioned for Zocha to sit and told her I would serve the drinks. This small gesture seemed to please her greatly.

"Good news and bad news," Filip said once we were all seated. "The police said they would drop the serious charges."

"Filip!" Zocha took his face in her hand as she had done with me only moments before. The happy lines around her eyes came back.

"Wait, there's more," said Tasha quietly.

We all heard the dread in Tasha's voice, and Zocha's smile lines disappeared.

Filip continued, "They will drop the serious charges if I take responsibility for what I did and agree to pay for all the damages."

"What do you mean for what you did?" asked Zocha.

"I guess Mr. and Mrs. Gowler talked to the prosecutor and asked for lesser charges. My lawyer said the Gowlers were worried about me. They are angry, but they said they wanted me to get help. So if I say I did it and pay for their car repairs, the prosecutor will only charge me with a misdemeanor. I'd have to go to counseling and have to do a lot of community service. If I refuse this offer, the charges stick and the prosecutor is going for the maximum penalty. He wants to press for juvenile detention because of the threats. All I have to do is say I did it."

"Which you are not going to do," Zocha said firmly.

"But what else is there?" asked Filip, frustrated. He looked at Tasha, "You heard the lawyer; I don't have a chance of winning this case."

"You didn't do what they say you did," said Zocha.

"No, but if I say I did it I can stay out of juvenile detention. That's a bonus, right?" I had never heard Filip talk with such anger.

Zocha looked at Filip without her usual warmth. "The bonus? That is not a bonus. So you will lie?"

"Grandma, I don't want to, but what else is there?"

"So you will lie and then expect all of us here to keep quiet about it?"

"Grandma, there isn't anything else to do."

She sighed and although the smile lines did not return, her gentleness did. "There is always something else, my love. It always seems easier to lie. But don't be mistaken. It is never as simple as it first seems. Lies and silence are brothers, they seem so innocent on the surface, but they will devour you."

"This is devouring me, too." He was yelling now. "I don't understand what you want me to do. If I don't lie, Grandma, they want to send me to juvenile detention. Juvenile detention! This is bigger than just getting kicked out of En-Gin-Unity. This is bigger than just a trip to the principal's office. This is juvenile detention. This is my life." Filip's voice was shaking, and both Tasha and I looked away to give him a small piece of privacy. It sounded like he was going to cry. "I don't want to go to juvenile detention."

"Oh darling, I don't want that either, but this won't be as simple as you think. Filip, you are telling yourself that there is no other way but to lie. You are telling yourself it will be simple to take the blame and then everything will be okay.

Deep down you know better than to do this. Telling yourself that is like inviting a wolf for breakfast and then being surprised when he decides to eat you instead of the biscuits." She laughed at herself and then walked over to Filip and gently lifted his chin to meet her gaze. "I know too much about these brothers of silence and lies," she said. "Make the wise choice and walk away from them, my love, and beware of the lies you tell yourself. I do not want to see you hurt more than you already are."

"But if he doesn't lie, he'll still be hurt," I cut in. I knew it wasn't the right thing to say. But it all felt so wrong and unfair. "It feels like he'll be hurt less if he decides to lie. At least he won't go to juvenile detention."

"Yes, it does seem that way," she said. "But you don't really know the outcome if Filip lies. You don't know what other danger that could bring."

"Both choices could end with something bad," I said angrily. "If he doesn't lie, that doesn't mean everything will be okay. He could still go to juvenile detention."

"Yes, this is true," said Zocha.

I wanted her to say that if he did the right thing, nothing bad would happen. But she didn't.

"I'm sorry, Zocha," I said, feeling bad for raising my voice. "I'm not upset with you, I'm upset with this situation."

"I understand," said Zocha. "I am upset too. You are right; we don't know the outcome of either lying or telling the truth. But, you must know that you are responsible for how you act—even when life is hard—you are still responsible. I see so many people blaming life when really it's their poor decisions."

She looked hard at Filip. "In the end, you take responsibility for what you choose here. You are responsible. If you lie, you may not blame the Gowlers for that poor decision. Your lie is on you."

We sat in silence for some time before Filip said, "I won't do it. I won't lie."

Zocha let out a long breath. Filip looked at Tasha and me and said, "Please, don't give up on me now."

I thought about what Maya had said to me—that I was in over my head. At that moment nothing felt more true. We were all in over our heads.

"We won't," said Tasha. "We're not going anywhere."

I can't tell you how much I respect Tasha for her cool head and calm temper. I wished I could be more like her and reassure Filip. But inside I was still simmering with frustration. "This whole thing still makes me angry," I said.

"I know, my dear," said Zocha. "It makes me angry too." And she did know; I could see it in her face. I suddenly had the feeling if we could pour out the contents of Zocha's heart, it would be full of heavy and sharp things—iron and jagged edges. And it seemed so strange to me that this soft loving woman could have things like that inside of her. We never really can tell what is in the heart of another person.

Seven

IN BLACK AND WHITE

After our meeting at Filip's, Tasha and I went home to get a good night's sleep before meeting again the next morning. Even though it was Saturday, I got up early and finished a math assignment I had been putting off for two days. I wanted to be able to devote the entire day to working on the case.

We met at our detective office at nine. Tasha had thought to bring bagels and juice, so we sat down at the desk and brainstormed over breakfast.

"What if we contact the university?" Tasha asked. "What if we explain the situation and ask them if they'll make an exception for Filip? Maybe he can sign something that says if he is found guilty he has to return the prize money."

"That's perfect," I said. "I mean, the charges are only pending. Maybe they'll be okay with that."

We found the contact information on the university's website and spent the next hour composing the perfect email. We explained Filip's dilemma and asked if we could set up a meeting between the head of the competition and Filip so he could explain his side of the story. Once it was complete we sat back and just stared at the screen, admiring our work. After a nod from Tasha, I hit send. It felt wonderful. It felt like hope.

"So now what?" I asked.

"I don't think we should just wait for a response. Let's keep brainstorming while we wait."

"What if we called the police station?" I asked. "What if we talked to the detective on the case to see if he can keep digging to prove Filip's innocence?"

I could tell Tasha wasn't completely on board with the idea, but I think she was starting to feel as desperate as I felt for something, anything that could help Filip.

We found the detective's name on the police report, and I dialed the number to the police station and asked for Detective Clauge. Tasha agreed to do the talking, but she put her phone on speaker so we could both hear.

"Detective Clauge," said the voice on the phone.

"Hi Detective Clauge," Tasha began. "My name is Tasha Winthrop, and I am helping Filip Basara with his case."

Silence.

She kept going. "My partner and I have been investigating, and we are convinced Filip is innocent. We are wondering if you could take the time to go back out to Tenebray and see if you missed anything."

"How old are you?" Detective Clauge asked.

"Thirteen," answered Tasha. "But sir, we are really concerned that he has been falsely accused."

"I see," he said. "Do you have any proof of that?"

"Well, no," answered Tasha.

"Do you have any new evidence?"

"No," admitted Tasha.

"So what exactly convinced you?" he asked.

"I guess it is just a feeling. We know Filip...."

Detective Clauge interrupted, "I'm sorry Miss Winthrop, but I need more than a feeling. If you have any real evidence to offer in the future, you may file a report with the front desk." He was obviously irritated.

"But sir," Tasha prodded, "Did you take fingerprints? Maybe you missed something? Or how about the woods? Did you find the spray paint that was used to write the message? Maybe you could trace that back to something."

"Miss Winthrop," His voice was stern now. "I am not at liberty to discuss this case, our investigation, or the written messages with you. Thank you for calling." The line clicked and went dead. He hung up on us.

Tasha looked at me. "Sorry, I tried."

"It's not your fault," I said. "I guess I was silly to think he'd talk to us."

Tasha's computer dinged with a new email message. It had a university address. "Open it," I whispered. I don't know why I whispered—maybe I just didn't want to break the small, hopeful moment. Tasha clicked on the message.

Dear Miss Winthrop,

Thank you for writing. I understand your concerns with the Filip Basara case. However, in order to run a fair and orderly contest, all contestants must follow the same application process. If Mr. Basara is cleared, he will be welcome to compete next year.

Thank you,
En-Gin-Unity Judging Panel

"But next year it will be a different contest and everything he worked for will be wasted!"

Tasha shut her computer and didn't say a thing.

"Why won't anyone help us?" I asked.

"I don't know," Tasha said quietly.

There's another difference between Tasha and me. One time I asked her why she never got angry about anything. She said she does get angry, but that her anger just looks different than mine. My anger, like most of my emotions, kind of bursts out of me, like when you open one of those pop-up books. Tasha's anger looks quiet. And if you didn't know her well, you'd think she didn't care. But she does; she's just trying to figure it all out in her head.

I offered to go inside and make us some lunch so she could think things through. She nodded, as if words would have disrupted her thoughts.

I only made it to the door before she said, "Wasn't there some big fuss when Tenebray became a national forest? Wasn't there a group who was angry that people were allowed to stay and live in the forest?"

"I have no idea," I answered, "That was like a gazillion years ago."

"Sixty years ago," she clarified. "I remember learning that in school or somewhere." She opened her laptop and entered a search for *Tenebray* and *protests*. She clicked on the first link, which showed a copy of an old news article.

August 19, 1952, Tenebray National Forest.

The dedication of the forest was met today with protests from the Tenebray Wildlife Group. They held signs claiming that the twelve remaining homes would compromise the integrity of the forest. Two protestors were arrested after making threats against the remaining residents of Tenebray Forest.

Tasha clicked on a link of pictures and one by one we viewed black and white photographs of the Tenebray dedication. There was a picture of a man on a podium. There was a picture of a woman cutting a ribbon near an entrance to the forest. We then viewed photos of the protest. There were about ten people holding signs that read things like, "Save the forest!" and "No homes in Tenebray!" The last two pictures showed police officers arresting two men.

Something caught my eye, but Tasha was clicking through the photos so fast that my mind only made sense of it after she moved on to another page. "Wait!" I yelled. "Go back. Go back to the second to last picture."

Tasha clicked back.

"Can you make it bigger?" I asked.

Tasha increased the size of the photo. She gasped when she saw it. The picture was of the police officers arresting the two protestors. The protestors had been handcuffed behind their backs. One of the protestor's signs had fallen to the ground and was lying so the words looked upside down in the photo. But the text was clear: *Leave or else.*

Eight

....
THE ONLY THING WE'VE GOT

"**W**hat are the chances that the same threatening message was used in Tenebray Forest sixty years ago?" Tasha asked.

"Not very good," I answered. "This was no coincidence. This is evidence. Let's call Detective Clauge."

"And tell him what?" Tasha asked. "It doesn't prove anything. I mean, look how easily we found the photo. Anyone else could have found it—including Filip. And it probably makes Filip look worse if they think he planned this out as some sort of retaliation for the 1952 arrests."

She was right. We had this big clue sitting right in front of us and it meant absolutely nothing. Tasha clicked on the *Contact Us* page near the photos. The website belonged to the Tenebray Historical Society. Tasha scrolled down until she found a name. "Joshua Allsburg, Director," she read.

"What are you thinking?" I asked.

"Monday after school we are going to their office to find out more information about the 1952 protest and more about the two men who were arrested."

"The competition deadline is Monday," I said. "We'll never find anything in time."

"Filip can email the forms until midnight. I'm sure Ms. Morely would email the recommendation if we can get him cleared." Tasha closed her computer. "That could be enough time to find something. Besides," she said in a flat voice, "right now, it's the only thing we've got."

Nine

....

NOTHING MATTERS

The next day was Sunday. Zocha invited us to church, and afterward we all returned to their house for lunch. Once there, Zocha led us to the kitchen and assigned us different tasks. First she led me to the stove where she had laid the ingredients for hot chocolate.

"Do you remember how to make it?" she asked.

"I've cemented it in my brain," I said. "I don't plan on ever forgetting something that good."

Zocha smiled and patted my cheek lovingly. She started Tasha on the salad and instructed Filip to mash the potatoes.

Once we were all comfortable with our tasks, Zocha tended to the meat, a chicken that had been roasting all morning. It smelled rich and warm and made the kitchen feel cozy.

"You eat chicken?" I joked with Zocha when she opened the oven to check it. "What would Ania say?"

Zocha pretended to be horrified, and I remembered what she had said about being dramatic as a kid. "Oh, my darling Ania. I'm sorry that I cooked your friend. Will you ever forgive me, my darling?"

Filip shook his head and laughed. "That's my grandma," he said. "Gotta love her."

It was nice, working all together like that. Somehow in that hour we spent in the kitchen, everything was normal. I don't think I even thought about Filip's case. We just laughed, and once all of our jobs were finished we set the table together. We felt like a little family.

The lunch conversation was easy and light. We didn't even discuss the case. Tasha and I talked about how we started the detective agency. Everyone laughed when Tasha told the story of how her very first case had been when she was five years old and her dad's socks and underwear kept ending up in the tree (Tasha discovered it was a squirrel, robbing the clothesline to build a nest). And Filip and Zocha took turns teaching us Polish words.

When we finished eating, we cleaned up, much like we had made the meal—together. For the first time in my life, doing the dishes was actually fun. Then we poured the mugs of hot chocolate and carried them to the living room. Zocha set a plate of cookies on the coffee table and we all fell into a content silence as we ate.

"Funny," I finally said, "we never would have gotten to know each other if it hadn't been for...." I immediately felt bad for saying it. We were having such a wonderful time and I felt like my words were going to push us back into reality and frustration.

But Zocha didn't seem frustrated at all. "Funny how it is with life," she said. "I would never wish for this to happen to Filip. Yet, I would never want to give up knowing you sweet girls. Perhaps life is never simple."

Tasha began to tell Filip and Zocha about the 1952 protests and about the photograph. I watched their faces as she talked; they all looked so hopeful. I tried so hard to push what I was feeling back inside. I tried to push it down and recreate the peace and happiness we had enjoyed all day. I wanted that back, but the other feeling was too strong. I could tell they all had the one thing I didn't have. They had hope.

I don't know exactly what I had. It wasn't quite anger or frustration — it seemed worse than that. And then the word came to me: despair. It was a word my English teacher had used once to describe a main character in a book. Despair, the absence of hope.

"It's over."

Everyone stopped talking and looked at me.

"Filip, I'm sorry," I said. "We failed, and I think we need to admit that. Nobody will help us and I don't know why. Nobody will listen. Nobody seems to care. And I don't know what else to do." My voice was shaking, but I didn't want to cry in front of everyone, so I clenched my teeth and swallowed hard before I continued. "The deadline is tomorrow and there is nothing to do. Nothing we did mattered." I couldn't stop the tears now. "Maya said I was in over my head. She's right. This is too big for us. This is too big for me. I'm sorry, Filip," I said. "I'm so sorry." And I must have said it ten more times. "I'm so sorry. I'm so sorry, I'm so sorry."

Ten

....

THE TRAINS

"I will never forget the sound of the trains."

At some point while saying how sorry I was, Tasha, Zocha, and Filip all moved toward me. Zocha sat next to me on the couch. Tasha sat at my feet, and Filip sat on the other side of me. We must have looked like birds huddled together in a nest.

Zocha didn't mention my tears or tell me to stop. She just said, "I will never forget the sound of the trains."

I didn't know what she meant, but from the way Filip

inhaled behind me, I knew that what she was saying would be important.

"When I was nine years old," she began, "the Nazi army invaded Poland. Our army tried to fight back, but we weren't strong enough. The Nazis were like a giant machine, a monster that seemed bigger than any of us. Our army was nothing for them, and soon they began rounding up innocent people and taking them away to prison camps. They took men, women, and even children. Children. Imagine that, they took children. It was a horrible time.

"My family lived in the countryside, far out from the city, but no place was safe. They were everywhere. We were farmers, and we were expected to give them our food. They didn't care if we had enough to eat. They felt they had the first rights to everything.

"A train track sliced through one of my father's fields. I grew up with the noise of the train. It's funny because before the war, my friends would come over and always complain about how loud the train was. I couldn't imagine what they were talking about. I knew the sound so well I didn't hear it anymore.

"But after the Nazis came, we found out they were using trains to bring people to the horrible prison camps. They'd load the people—their prisoners—in cattle cars and take them away. And it was like the horror of it made me suddenly realize how loud the train really was—the scream of the steam, the scraping of the metal, the bumping of the cars on the tracks.

"We all knew those trains were full of innocent people being taken away. But we couldn't say anything or do anything. My father wouldn't even look at the trains, and he told us not to look either. He wasn't being cold; you mustn't think my father was a cold man. He was afraid. If the Nazis even thought we were against them they would take us as prisoners, too. They didn't need proof; it could be as simple as looking at a soldier the wrong way. My father wasn't cold. He wasn't a coward. He was just trying his best to keep his children safe.

"I was only a child. But it still haunts me, more than seventy years later. We were all so afraid, and we all felt so helpless. What were we supposed to do? How could we have stopped a barreling train? I don't know. If the answer was easy, we'd all have done it.

"Then one day I was working in the field near the tracks. I saw something move in the long grass and I walked toward it, expecting to find a wounded animal. As I got closer I realized that it wasn't an animal at all. It was a child. He was about two years old, just tall enough for his head to stick above the long grass. He was very dirty and he was holding his arm, which was obviously broken. The odd thing was that he was silent. You'd expect a child that age to cry, but he didn't. He looked up at me with such fear. I suppose I looked just as afraid as he did.

"You see, we had all heard the stories, so when I saw that child with a broken arm sitting near the tracks, I could guess where he had come from. We had heard that a few times the adult prisoners on the train were able to pry open a part of the cattle car—just a small space, just enough to push a child out. It sounds cruel when I say it, doesn't it? Who would think to throw a child from a train? But it wasn't cruel. They were giving their children the only chance there was to escape and be free. When I say life is never simple, it isn't. Imagine being a parent and the only hope you have left to save your child is to throw him from the train. It must have been excruciating for those parents.

"The child and I just looked at each other and then I walked toward him, picked him up as gently as I could, and carried him to my house.

"When I walked through the door my mother's face was as if she had seen a ghost. I knew what she was thinking. I was thinking it, too. If we were caught with this child, our whole family would be arrested and put on a train. Helping this child meant risking our lives. But my mother just walked to me and took the child from my arms. She kissed his forehead the way she always kissed us.

"My mother told me to get some of my younger brother's clothes, and she gently bathed the boy and dressed him. She sent me outside to find proper sticks, and she ripped cloth to make a splint for his arm. She gave him something to eat.

"My whole family could have been arrested for what I had done. But no matter how I tried to turn it around in my mind, leaving him lying in the grass wasn't right. You remember how I said to beware of the lies you tell yourself?"

I nodded.

"Convincing myself to leave him lying there would have been one of those lies. The longer I stood there the more I realized that leaving that child in the grass and doing nothing was what the Nazis needed. Silence fed their machine. They depended on our silence to make them stronger. And that made me angry. They had tried so hard to break us with their cruelty. Maybe they thought if they were cruel to us, we'd become cruel to one another. I don't know what they thought, but I refused to be like them.

"We didn't have a place to hide him so my father went to our neighbor, who had created a secret cellar under his home. Our neighbor used the cellar mostly to hide food, money, jewelry—things they didn't want the Nazis to take. My father asked them to hide the child in their cellar. You remember how I said my father was not a coward?"

We nodded.

"You need to understand what a very risky thing it was for my father to go to the neighbor for help. He was putting himself in great danger just by asking. The Nazis gave rewards for information on people. So our neighbors could have turned us in and made a great deal of money."

"Did your father know he would say yes?" I asked.

"My father *hoped* he'd say yes."

"What happened?" asked Tasha.

"My father returned home and told us that the neighbors had been very afraid of taking in the boy, but they agreed. So that night, my mother wrapped the child in a blanket. We placed the boy in a wheelbarrow and my mother covered him with another thick blanket. We then covered him in sticks and small pieces of firewood. When the boy was hidden, my father wheeled the child to the neighbor's house. He said the short walk felt like the longest walk of his life. One could never be sure who was watching."

"Did your father make it?" I asked.

"Yes. It was a miracle that a boy that small knew how to stay hidden and still."

"What happened to the boy?" I asked.

"My neighbors spent two years hiding and caring for the boy. After the war, they raised him as their son."

Zocha turned her body to face me. "I know what it is to feel small and helpless. Maybe you won't meet the deadline. Maybe Filip won't be in the contest. But that doesn't mean we give up. I tell you this because I lived it.

"Not one of us could overthrow that machine that invaded my country. But each small act of resistance put a crack in it. We had to stop being overwhelmed by how big it was because that is just how life is, my dear. It is always too big and we always feel too small. And we don't act because we convince ourselves that our small act won't even make a dent. Yet, my dears, there are so many moving pieces all the time, so many things that are bigger than us. Doing something to correct injustice is never wasted. You never know where your piece falls in. Your job isn't to do everything. My job wasn't to do it all, it was simply to carry a boy out of the grass."

After many hugs, Tasha and I left Zocha and Filip's house. Tasha walked me home. The leftover warmth of summer was gone and the first true autumn wind of the season was blowing. We didn't say much as we walked. I think we both felt heavy. How could someone as sweet as Zocha come from all that pain? Like I said before, you never really can tell what is in the heart of another person.

I went to bed around midnight. I stayed up late to finish a paper for English and to study for my math test. I had spent every bit of my spare time on the Tenebray case, and for the last few days it was as if giving up sleep was the only option to find enough hours in the day to go to school, help Filip, and keep my grades up. It had been exhausting. I printed my paper and closed my computer. My bed had never felt so good. My body seemed to melt into the mattress. But, as much as I wanted to sleep, as exhausted as my body felt, my mind wouldn't turn off. Every time I closed my eyes I imagined Filip in juvenile detention. I imagined what would have happened if Zocha had been caught by the Nazis. It was as if the quiet night had brought every fear I have ever had to the surface. I pulled my blankets up to my chin and wished I had opened my bedroom door before I went to bed.

I reminded myself that everything that was going through my mind was untrue. Zocha hadn't been caught and Filip wasn't in juvenile detention, not yet anyway. I knew that more than anything I just needed sleep so my mind was fresh. And my self-talk almost worked. My body relaxed and my breathing slowed, but just as I was in that delicate place between waking and sleeping an image came to my mind. I very clearly remembered the eyes that had been watching us that first day in Tenebray Forest. And in my dark and quiet room, I could no longer rationalize my way out of it. I knew what I saw. I knew what was true. Someone had been stalking us.

Eleven

ON THE EDGE OF NIGHT

"We need to go back to the woods," I said as we walked to school. "Today."

"Why?" asked Tasha.

I told Tasha about the eyes and how I saw something red and how even though I couldn't explain it I knew it was important, and I knew we had to go.

"Okay," she said. "I believe you. But we can't today. This morning I was able to arrange a meeting with Joshua Allsburg at the Historical Society. We have to be there right after school."

My chest felt tight. It was time to go back into Tenebray. Something in my gut told me it was urgent—that this was one of those things that couldn't wait. "Then how about you go talk to Mr. Allsburg and I'll go check out Tenebray."

"Chloe," said Tasha, "I'm not sure that's such a great idea."

"Of course it's not," I said. "But right now we don't have time for perfect ideas. Filip's deadline is today. We need to split up to cover everything, otherwise we'll never get it done in time."

Tasha thought for a moment. She is very organized and likes to do everything without risk, by the book. Splitting up was not something she liked.

"No, Chloe," she finally said. "You know better than being out in the forest alone."

"Tasha…." I started to argue.

"No," she said firmly. "After the Historical Society we can go to the woods together."

"Tasha…." I tried one more time.

"Chloe," she interrupted, "please."

She looked so worried that I gave in.

The day dragged. I couldn't stop looking at the clock. I think it moved in slow motion. When the bell rang at 2:30, I met Tasha in the hall and walked with her to the Historical Society. As we walked we went over questions for the director. Then we went over everything we knew about the evidence just in case we missed something. As we were about to enter the Historical Society I saw Elsie turning down the street.

"Tash," I said, "It's Elsie. I'm sure she's walking home. I can walk with her—her dad always waits for her and walks her through the woods. You can do the Historical Society, and I can do the forest. We'll save time, and I'll be safe."

"I don't' know, Chloe."

"Come on, Tash. The deadline is tonight and I'll be with Mr. Gowler. All I need to do is walk to that spot. I'll ask him first if he'll walk me back out. Besides, it will give me a chance to talk to Elsie again."

Tasha didn't look pleased, but she said, "You promise to stay with Elsie and her dad?"

"Of course."

"Okay, I guess that's safe. Take your phone and call me as soon as you are done." She gave me a hug and whispered, "Be safe," in my ear. I gave her one last squeeze and turned to catch up with Elsie.

"Chloe," Tasha called from behind me. "Be careful."

I know Elsie saw me, but she kept walking. I called her name, but she wouldn't turn around. Finally I ran up next to her and tapped her on the shoulder.

"Why are you ignoring me?" I asked.

"I didn't hear you," she said, but, of course, that was a lie.

"Can I walk with you?" I asked.

She didn't say anything.

"I just need to look for something in the forest, but I don't want to go in alone. Can I walk with you?"

As I was talking she pulled an iPod out of her backpack. "I really can't," she said. "I have a Spanish test tomorrow, and I need to listen to this to learn it."

So much for talking. "That's okay," I said. "I won't bother you; I'll just walk."

She looked either worried or irritated, I couldn't quite tell. But she didn't tell me to leave her alone, so that was good. She put in her earbuds, and we walked in silence.

When we got closer to the forest, Elsie took off her earbuds and said, "What are you looking for? My dad isn't going to like you snooping around."

"Why not?" I asked.

"He just won't. Besides, the Dodds really won't like it."

I thought about the Dodd stories, about how they never left the woods, about how strange they were. *Crazy,* some people said. "Well, I'm not going on the Dodd's land; I just want to look around on forest property. That doesn't belong to anyone."

"The Dodds think it all belongs to them."

"Elsie," I said, "I know Maya thinks she saw Filip, but what if it was someone else? For instance, what if it was Andrew Dodd? Maybe they look alike."

"My dad meets me at the entrance to the forest," she said. "I do not want to talk about this around him."

"Why not?" I asked, perplexed.

"It upsets him."

I thought about the easygoing man we had met a few days ago and it was hard to imagine him upset.

"Maybe you should turn around," she said.

I was getting irritated. "No, Elsie. I'm not going home. I don't know what you are hiding, but...."

"I'm not hiding anything!" she yelled.

"Then why are you afraid to let me go into the forest?"

"I'm not afraid of anything," she said. "If you want to go into the forest, fine. Go."

I felt exhausted again. I hate being yelled at. And the worst part was that this was so unlike Elsie. Last year, a new kid started at school and it was Elsie who went out of her way to make sure everyone was kind to her. It was Elsie who sat with her at lunch, introduced her to her friends, and even helped her join the track team. I didn't understand what had changed. What had made this once-sweet person become rude and mean?

Mr. Gowler waved to us from the two-track.

"Wait here while I go talk to him," she said.

"Talk to him about what?" I asked. But she had already started walking away from me. For a moment, I thought she was going to ditch me, but after she talked to her dad for a few minutes, she walked back to me.

"You can follow us into the forest. But my dad doesn't want to talk to you either."

"What? Why? Elsie, what did you tell him?" What kind of lies was she telling about me?

"Look, if you want to find your thing in the forest, that's the deal. Got it?"

"I guess," I answered.

"Let us get a head start. You can keep us in your sights, so you are safe, but don't catch up to us. Got it?" she asked again.

I nodded, but I was still completely confused as to how someone as kind and sweet as Elsie could switch so quickly into someone so mean. And then I had an epiphany. Elsie had something to hide.

As instructed, I waited for Elsie and her dad to get a head start before I walked to the two-track and the tunnel-like opening to the forest. Fear is a funny thing. It seemed to crawl up my body like a million tiny bugs. I rubbed the back of my neck to try to undo the prickly feeling that coursed up my spine. It was no use. I had heard the expression, *paralyzed by fear,* but until that point I didn't really understand it. Now I did. Now I was paralyzed. No matter how hard I tried, I couldn't seem to move my feet forward into the opening of the forest.

I could see Elsie and her father up ahead of me. Elsie might have been mean to me, but I knew they would never hurt me. I remembered Mr. Gowler's insistence that he escort us out of the forest, and I felt safe in his adult presence.

Once the fear subsided, I had to battle another feeling: exhaustion. I just didn't want to do this anymore. I hadn't slept much over the weekend. I was tired. I was hungry. I just wanted to go home. I wanted to be a normal kid. I wanted everything that was not this.

And then I thought of Zocha. Before we left her house yesterday, I had asked her the question that had baffled me from the beginning. "Why us?"

Without pause Zocha replied, "Because you were the only ones who would listen."

I thought of Zocha as a young girl standing over that child. I couldn't imagine what type of fear she had to overcome or what she risked to pick up that boy. But she did it anyway. I wanted to be like her, this tender woman with nerves of steel. If Zocha could carry a boy out of the grass, I could go back into Tenebray Forest.

I thought then how funny our lives are—how they wrap around each other and stretch far through time. I thought about how a girl carrying a boy out of some grass seventy years earlier could motivate me to go into Tenebray. I realized then, on the edge of the dark forest, that our lives and the things we do are much greater than we often think.

The first step was the hardest—the step out of the sunlight and into the dark forest. The shadows enveloped me at once. The roaring silence of nature once again surrounded me and dried pine needles, dappled with light, crunched under each step. Once I was in, it was easy to keep going. I followed the two-track into the woods, keeping Elsie and her dad in my sight. Finally, I recognized the long Y-shaped tree. I slowly turned in a circle, looking for something red. Nothing. I immediately began to doubt myself. What if it had been a cardinal? What if I hadn't really seen anything at all?

I could still see Elsie and her dad. Even though they were far ahead, the track was straight for a while, so I figured I had time to explore a bit before they were out of my sight. I left the two-track and carefully stepped into the woods. It wasn't easy. The underbrush was thick and tangled. I walked in the direction of where I had seen the eyes.

I stopped at where I thought I had seen the eyes and the red something. Again I turned in a circle to look around. I wondered if what I had seen was paper. If it was paper it could have blown. It certainly wouldn't have blown far with the thick underbrush, but I knew I had to widen my search. I looked behind to the two-track. As long as I had it in my sight, I knew I couldn't get lost. I felt, deep in my stomach, that that piece of red meant something, and I needed to find it.

I realized that the light was fading, and I remembered the warnings of night falling earlier in the forest. I started crisscrossing back and forth deeper into the forest. I figured if I maintained some sort of pattern in my steps, I could easily retrace them back to the two-track. The farther I went, the more difficult it was to see. I looked at my phone. It was almost five o'clock and the sun had dropped below the tree line so everything in the forest was losing light.

Then I saw it. Something red was lying on a bush about twenty feet ahead. It hadn't been a bird or my imagination. It was right there. The forest had become so thick that I practically had to rip through the vines and branches and brush to reach the splotch of red. I picked it up. It was a label for spray paint, which I took to mean that whoever had spray painted the Gowler's car had been here to hide the evidence. I was sure the rest of it was around here somewhere. All I had to do was search for something unusual on the forest floor like a freshly dug hole or a patch of pressed down foliage.

By now the light was nothing more than a dim glow. I chose a direction and walked. When it didn't pan out, I chose a different direction. When that didn't pan out I chose another. And that's when I saw it. There was a space of bare earth, the only spot like it. I knelt down over the space and began digging with my hands. I only had to dig about a foot deep before I felt a plastic bag. I dug around the edges and finally was able to pull up a trash bag. Inside I found plastic gloves, covered in paint, and three used cans of spray paint in the same colors that had been used to vandalize the car. Detective Clauge wanted new evidence? I had new evidence.

Twelve

DARKNESS

Most of the time it is the tourists who get lost in Tenebray Forest—someone from out of town ventures too far on a hike without understanding how disorienting the thick trees can be. Those of us who have grown up next to Tenebray can't help but understand its power. The forest curves around our town like giant arms, and it is almost impossible not to feel small when you are near it. From the time we are little kids we are taught to respect the power of the forest. We even have a forest-safety course that all kindergarteners must complete. Ask the youngest child around Tenebray and he'll tell you that the important thing to do when you are lost in the forest is to stay in one spot and wait for someone to find you. When you wander around it makes it harder for someone to rescue you, and you risk becoming further entangled in the vast and secluded forest.

So I should have known better. One thing I'm certain of, if Tasha had been with me, it never would have happened. She's much too cautious to make a mistake like that. She is never impulsive like I am.

I gently folded the bag and put it in my backpack. I stood, eager to leave the woods before night completely swallowed the forest. That was when I realized I was lost. I had been so intent on finding something on the ground that I hadn't kept track of where I was. I had lost all direction. Tenebray Forest was more than forty miles of trees and brush. If I started walking in the wrong direction, I knew it was possible I'd never find my way out.

I looked at my phone, but there was no signal. I sank to my knees. It felt like the whole forest had taken two steps closer to me and was pressing against my chest. I couldn't breath; I couldn't think. It was hard not to cry. I had never felt so trapped or so alone. The setting sun took its warmth with it. I could see my breath in the air. As if to announce all my troubles at once, my stomach growled.

Tasha and I had always taken our business very seriously. We read endless books and articles about being a good detective and how to notice and find clues. We read books on interviewing suspects and we practiced interviewing each other. We wanted to be good at what we did so we tried to think of everything. But here I was. Zocha was right when she had said there just wasn't enough straw to soften all the bad things that happen to us.

And hadn't the same thing happened to Filip? Hadn't he done everything right? And yet everything was taken from him. Hadn't Zocha's family done what was right? Yet the Nazis took over their country and their lives. And it seemed to me that no matter how hard we try to prepare for life, at some moment the wrong turn down the wrong path or someone else's bad decision can leave us completely unprepared and completely lost.

I don't know how long I crouched there on the forest floor. I sat there long enough to think about every unfair circumstance I could. The more I brooded, the lower I sank, the colder I became, and the more hopeless I felt.

I looked up at all the trees around me. The forest was so big. I was never going to find my way out. And just like that I thought of something Zocha had said.

Not one of us could overthrow that machine that invaded my country. But each small act of resistance put a crack in it. We had to stop being overwhelmed by how big it was because that is just how life is, my dear. It is always too big and we always feel too small.

Like water to a drooping plant, I felt reenergized.

I wasn't going to find my way out. I knew this. But someone would come looking. When I didn't come home, my parents would call Tasha and she knew where I had gone. That gave me hope to crack my despair. I knew I simply needed to do one thing: survive in the forest until I was found. I didn't have much hope of finding food in the dim light, but that was the least of my worries. I was looking at spending the night alone in Tenebray Forest. I knew that complete darkness would soon move in and I had to act fast while I still had dim light. I knew I had to find or build some sort of shelter.

Through the shadows I could see a small broken tree branch on the ground. I picked it up and placed one end in the crook of another tree. I had once watched my dad build a small lean-to, and I was pretty sure I could mimic a rough version of what he had made. I found smaller branches and leaned them on the larger branch to create a kind of tent. I worked quickly to gather as many fallen leaves and pine needles as I could and place them on the bottom of my shelter. I figured some padding would keep me away from the cold ground and keep me warmer. By the time I finished I needed to use the light from my phone to find the small opening. I crawled in and used a few small sticks I had gathered to close the opening. While my shelter was fragile and no match for a bear or cougar, it did offer enough security to make me feel somewhat safer than what I'd be just sitting in the middle of the forest. I took off my backpack and used it for a pillow.

I thought I understood darkness before that night, but this was something totally different. I couldn't see my hand just inches from my nose. It was a scary feeling to see no difference from my opened or closed eyes. It made the darkness feel like an object, heavy and suffocating. I had to fight the urge to stay still, and every once in a while I allowed myself to turn on my cell phone, just for a glimpse of light.

I couldn't sleep. I thought about how luxurious it would be if I could just fall asleep and wake up to sunshine and light, and how wonderful it would be if I could just sleep through this scary night. But no matter how hard I tried to relax, I was simply too afraid to close my eyes. Instead, I made a game of trying to see the first light of dawn.

Then I heard a crack. Something was near my lean-to. I didn't dare move or turn on my light. I even tried to slow my breathing. My heart was beating so hard I was sure whatever was out there could hear it.

"Dear God," I prayed, *"please don't leave me."*

CRACK. CRACK. CRACK. It was getting closer.

Thirteen

WOULD I KNOW WHERE I'D FALL

There was breathing. It wasn't mine. I tried to think of what nocturnal animals lived in the forest. Raccoons, skunks, but what about bears? Were bears nocturnal? Cougars? Wolves? Whatever was outside my lean-to wasn't human. It was snorting a bit and seemed to be foraging around on the ground. And for the first time since all of this started, I was thankful I hadn't brought food in my backpack. Whatever was out there would have certainly smelled food.

The animal seemed to be digging, and then it sounded like it lay down near my lean-to. Now and then I heard scratches on the ground, but mainly it was silent. My foot was asleep, but I didn't dare change positions for fear the animal would attack. But after a bit I realized that whatever it was, it had most likely already smelled me and was choosing to ignore me. Strangely, I started to feel safer with the creature outside my tent. Having another life nearby eased my loneliness. Then, despite my fear and despite being cold to the bone, I drifted into sleep.

I woke to birds, and when I opened my eyes it was just light enough to make out the outline of my shoes. I turned on my phone, but the face was blank. The battery had died in the night. I realized the forest would be lighter than inside my lean-to, so I gently moved a branch to peek outside. There was no sign of an animal. As I crawled out, I hoped that whatever had rested with me last night had left while I was sleeping.

It was day two in the forest. My mouth was dry, and I'm pretty sure that knowing I didn't have anything to drink increased my thirst. I stretched as I took in my surroundings. I hoped I would find something I missed in the dark. But every direction looked hopelessly the same. I knew that it was important for me not to wander. I knew I had the best chance of being rescued if I stayed put. But I also knew I needed food and, more importantly, I needed water. Tenebray was dense and large and I knew it could be days before I was found. I had to survive and that meant wandering at least to find food and water.

I chose a direction and started walking, but this time it was much more difficult. I was stiff and weak from thirst and hunger. I don't know how long I walked, but after a while I felt sick and dizzy. My head started swirling so I took off my pack and again used it as a pillow. I lay down on the ground and almost immediately fell asleep, my hunger and thirst and exhaustion now overpowered my fear.

I don't know how long I slept, but when I suddenly sat up, the air was warmer and the sun was directly overhead. I thought for a moment that something had awakened me, but I was too tired to even imagine anymore. The forest was full of noises, I told myself. I dozed off again.

When I awoke the second time, my head was pounding and the inside of my mouth was sticky. I considered chewing a leaf, but I wasn't sure which leaves were safe and which were poisonous. Last night I had been ambitious. I decided that I needed to get shelter, food, and water. But now my focus had narrowed. I needed water, only water. I pulled myself up by holding on to a tree trunk. I had to lean over for a moment until a swirl of dizziness passed.

CRACK.

I didn't even flinch. I guess looking back I knew the noise was louder and closer than it should have been. But I was so tired and my head hurt so much I just didn't care. I started walking.

CRACK.

I should have realized that someone or something was getting closer.

CRACK.

I looked ahead and saw what looked like a long clearing in the trees. Why hadn't I seen it before? For a moment I thought that maybe I had miraculously wandered back to the two-track, but as I got closer I could tell that the land had begun to slope. I smiled. Water flows down. Perhaps at the bottom of the slope was a creek. I needed water.

CRACK.

The fear crawled up my body to my neck. But I kept walking forward.

CRACK.

It was close behind me now.

CRACK.

I kept walking, ignoring the prickly feelings of fright.

CRACK.

I felt like I was being watched, but the forest plays tricks on your mind. Like the way a loud rustle in the underbrush is nothing but a small squirrel, or how you are sure you see a bear but then it turns out to be nothing more than the shadow of a branch. After a while it's hard to know what is real in the forest. I ended up dismissing everything—even the things I should have been afraid of.

Now it was too late.

The branches cracked behind me and I didn't have time to turn before I felt someone grab the back of my coat. The button on my coat dug into the center of my throat. I gagged and then slid backward through the thick, dried pine needles. Then I was down, sprawled on my back.

I started to cry. I didn't mean to cry, but I couldn't help it. It had all been too much. The tears streamed down my face and dripped into my ears. I realized one sharp pine needle had pierced the top of my thumb. I didn't even think to pull it out. I just looked up to the figure hovering over me, and I had one sure thought: you never know where you will fall.

Fourteen

....

THINGS ARE NOT AS THEY SEEM

"People are looking for you," he said as he hovered over me. He was wearing a heavy sweatshirt with a hood. It was hard to see his face.

I sat up, but a wave of nausea made it difficult to move. I tried to crawl away from him. He grabbed my arm, and as I began to fight I looked down. I was on the edge of a massive cliff. I had been right that the slope of the landscape led to a river. What I hadn't realized was that the river was located at the bottom of a hundred foot drop. The edge of the cliff was so overgrown that I knew if this person hadn't grabbed my shirt and later my arm, I would have certainly plummeted over the edge.

I stopped resisting and let him pull me back. Once we were away from the cliff's edge he let go, and I sat with my legs tucked under me.

"Are you hurt?" he asked, rather gruffly.

I shook my head. "Just thirsty."

He pulled a water bottle from his pack and tossed it toward me. I drank greedily.

"Sit for a few minutes, but then we need to move. We're so far in I'm not sure we'll be out before dark."

Was he helping me?

"Where's your friend?" he said.

"What friend?"

"She was out here with you the other day."

I thought of the cracking branch and the eyes. "Where are you taking me?" I asked.

He laughed. "Where am I taking you?" he asked back.

"I want to go home."

"Well I'm not taking you to my home," he said. "Let's get moving. I don't really want to spend the night in the forest."

"Well I don't either," I said.

He didn't answer, and I had to scramble up to follow him. He walked through the forest with ease, overstepping the underbrush and moving between the branches. I stumbled behind him, tripping over vines and bumping into branches. He never looked back or offered to help. Every once in a while he'd tell me to hurry up.

He scooted up a small embankment, but when I followed I slipped on some loose gravel and slipped back.

He turned, showing no pity, just irritation. "Come on, get up," he said.

"No." I answered. That was it. I was done. Here I was following some strange person through the woods in the hopes that he was helping me. But for all I knew, he was leading me deeper into the woods. I wasn't going to follow him another step.

"Suit yourself. Find your own way out." He didn't seem very bothered.

"You are just going to leave me here?" I protested.

"You said you weren't getting up." With that he turned and kept walking.

"Wait!" I screamed after him.

Surprisingly, he turned.

"I have been stuck in the woods for two days with nothing to eat or drink. Last night I slept in the forest next to some wild creature. I almost fell down a ravine. I'm tired. My head is pounding. I'm dizzy, and I don't know who you are or where you are taking me."

He looked at me, expressionless, and then said, "I'm Andrew. Are you coming now?"

"Where are you taking me?" I asked.

"I'm taking you back to the two-track."

"Why?"

"Would you rather I left you here?" he questioned.

I shook my head.

"Well, then can you please get up so we have a chance of getting out of here by dark?"

I nodded and stood up. This time he waited while I climbed the embankment. When I reached the top he said, "Stay closer to me. Follow my steps exactly; it will be easier."

We started walking, but I quickly fell behind, still tangled in the mess of forest. Then he stopped so abruptly that I bumped into him. He sighed and said, "You are looking everywhere but at my feet. Stop it."

"I need to look where I'm going," I protested.

"No you don't. I'm looking where we are going. You look at my feet and step where I step." He turned and started walking before I could answer.

He was right. I walked closely behind him and put my foot where he had taken the last step. I stopped stumbling.

"What were you doing in the woods?" I asked.

He didn't turn around but answered, "I live here. The better question is what were you doing in the woods?"

I remembered how Mr. Gowler had asked us that first day if we were there to see Elsie or Andrew. This was Andrew Dodd from the other house in Tenebray. He looked like he was about sixteen years old. I thought about all the stories I had heard about Andrew's family. They were crazy.

"I was looking for something," I answered.

"Did you find it?" he asked.

Somehow through my headache and exhaustion I was able to think clearly enough to realize that this person leading me out of the forest could very well be our number one suspect, and I wasn't about to tell him whether or not I found the evidence against him.

"How did you find me?" I asked, avoiding the question.

"It was pretty simple really. I heard this morning that you were missing. I hunt these woods almost daily, so I know them better than most people. I just followed your trail."

"How?" I asked.

"You left an easy trail for me to follow. When most people walk through the forest they don't think about where they are walking or what they are stepping on and crushing. Nice lean-to, by the way."

"Thanks," I said. I thought about the protests against the Tenebray homes. Hadn't they said that the homes ruined the forest? Andrew was talking about how most people were careless in the forest. Was this the connection? Was Andrew the vandal? It didn't make total sense though. If Andrew was against people living in the forest, why did he live in the forest? Maybe it was the way the Gowlers lived that angered Him. They had built a giant home and put in the paved driveway. Maybe he felt like his neighbors were ruining his peaceful forest. The light was dimming, and I knew from experience that it would be dark soon. The water had helped, but my stomach ached from hunger.

"Are we going to make it out before dark?" I asked.

"I don't know."

We kept walking and walking and with each step my head throbbed harder. I felt as if I could puke.

"We can keep going a bit longer, but stay close," he directed. "Did you find the spray paint?"

I stopped walking. He knew. I realized if I lost him, I'd lose my way out of the forest, so I quickened my steps to meet his. "Spray paint?" I asked.

"That's what you came here for, right? You found it, huh. It's in your backpack maybe?"

I didn't say anything.

"I thought so," he finally said.

"Why did you do it?" I asked.

He sighed. "You think I did it?"

"Did you?" I asked.

He shook his head. "That is so typical."

"What is that supposed to mean?" He was accusing me of something and it made me mad.

He answered with as much anger as I felt. "Of course Andrew did it. He's a Dodd, right? Isn't that what you are thinking? Those crazy Dodds, right? I mean, we don't live like the rest of you or dress like the rest of you so we must be nuts and crazy and evil, right?"

I couldn't think of a thing to say, so I just stared at him.

He continued, "And that's why you think I'm going to hurt you, right? Because I'm a Dodd?"

I shrugged, which plainly irritated him.

"A shrug?" he asked. "All I get is a shrug? Look, I didn't ruin the car, okay? And I didn't come here to hurt you. I tracked you because it's dangerous out here, and, contrary to what people think, I'm not crazy. In fact, when I heard about a girl lost in the forest, I was worried and I wanted to help." He started walking. "Look, are you coming?"

I nodded and started to follow him again.

"You want to know what happened to the car?" he said as he walked. "Try talking to Elsie and Maya."

"I did that," I said.

"Talk to them again."

That's when the doubt started. Was I wrong about Andrew? "Andrew?" I asked.

"What?"

"Look," I said, "I'm sorry. I'm tired and hungry and I wasn't thinking right. I'm sorry I accused you."

He stopped and I nearly bumped into him again. He turned and shook his head at me. "Your apology isn't accepted. If you are going to apologize, at least be truthful. This wasn't about you being hungry and tired. You think I did it because of all the things you've heard about my family."

He was right. I couldn't disagree; he was simply right. I've done lots of skimming apologies in my life—a quick *I'm sorry* or the *I'm sorry, but…* where you explain why the person deserved it. I think maybe this was the first time I was faced with a naked apology—one that wasn't covered in my excuses. He was right. I was wrong. It was a little scary to be in that position, to stand in front of someone and say, *You're right. I was wrong, and I've got no good reasons to give. I messed up.* Naked apologies are so much harder than the quick sorrys. Maybe it's harder because a naked apology feels like you are giving control to that person to determine if you are going to be forgiven or not.

I took a deep breath and was honest. "I thought you did it because I heard your family was crazy. That wasn't fair. And I figured you were going to hurt me for the same reason. I'm very sorry Andrew."

He looked at me for a long time. I was too afraid to look at him so instead I just stared at the ground. I was waiting for him to yell at me, or tell me how wrong I was, or how I hurt him, or how I needed to pay for what I did. But he just looked at me.

"Okay," he finally said. "Thank you. Now, let's keep going so we can get you home before dark."

"Thank you," I said. It probably sounded like I was thanking him for getting me home, but what I really meant was to thank him for forgiving me. He didn't have to and after being so honest and wrong in front of someone, forgiveness feels a little like that first drink I had from Andrew's bottle—it feels a little bit like coming back to life.

He smiled. "Sure, let's go."

We walked until the dark shadows completely swallowed the forest. I heard voices up ahead and small pricks of light through the trees. "There's your search party," said Andrew. "Walk toward the lights."

"Aren't you coming?" I asked. But I was talking to myself. Andrew had already disappeared into the shadows. He had saved me. The crazy boy from Tenebray Forest had led me out to safety. I thought of something Zocha had once said to me, *There is always more than you first see*.

Fifteen

DON'T TELL MY DAD

I stumbled onto the two-track, and for a moment it was strangely calm and quiet while the three men from the search party just stared at me. "Chloe?" one of them finally asked. I nodded and the silence was broken. One of them radioed in that they had found me. I could hear cheers over the radio. It was strange to know that those cheers were for me.

The men led me to the Gowler's house, and both of my parents ran down the driveway and enveloped me in their arms. We all cried. I don't know how long we stood there crying and holding each other, but I didn't want to let go. Finally my dad suggested I get something to eat. My mom held my hand and led me inside where the police had set up their search headquarters. I hadn't held my mom's hand for years, but I'll be honest, it felt really great. Once inside I noticed how swollen my parents' faces were. They had been crying a lot. "What were you thinking?" my dad kept asking. "What were you thinking?"

Tasha was there too, and her face was swollen as well. She embraced me and cried and kept saying how it was her fault, how she should have known better than to let me go. I hugged her tight and told her that none of it was her fault.

The police were there, and they wanted to ask me some questions about what had happened but suggested I eat first. Mrs. Gowler brought me a plate of a chicken and noodle casserole. I finished it in minutes and asked for seconds. Once I was full, the officer led me to the Gowler's living room and introduced me to a man wearing jeans and a polo shirt. "This is Detective Clauge," the officer said.

The detective motioned for me to sit on the couch, and he sat in a chair across from me. "I understand you were with the young girl who called me about the Filip Basara case."

I nodded.

"Would you like to tell me what is going on?"

I told him about Filip and how he had asked us to help him. I told him about the photographs we had discovered, and I told him about Andrew and how he helped me out of the forest. "I found the spray paint," I told him.

I explained where I'd found it and how I dug it up. He asked to see it and I pulled the bag from my backpack.

"Chloe," he said. "I had no idea those photographs existed. You are going to be a great detective some day." His praise felt like a warm blanket.

"However, he added, with an edge of disappointment in his voice, "I can't use the spray paint as evidence."

"Why?" I asked.

"You disturbed the evidence. Who's to say you didn't just make the whole thing up?"

The warm blanket of his praise was gone, and I felt the iciness of failure.

"You really believe Filip is innocent, don't you?" he asked.

"With all my heart."

"You shouldn't have gone into the forest," he said.

"I know."

He took a deep breath. "I'll keep looking," he answered. "But please, I'm going to have to ask you to refrain from disappearing into forests for a while." He smiled.

Someone was helping us. Finally, someone didn't brush us aside. Finally, we weren't totally alone in helping Filip.

"You'll drop the charges against Filip?" I asked hopefully.

"No. But I'll keep looking."

It wasn't much. But it was something.

He stood and briefly talked to my parents about how wonderful it was to have a happy ending in a missing person case. Tasha sat down next to me.

"Filip missed his En-Gin-Unity deadline, didn't he?" I asked.

She nodded.

"Is he okay?"

"He was more worried about you than about the competition. But he's definitely sad."

"I really thought I had something, but then I just lost track of where I was. If I had been paying attention maybe…."

Tasha put her arm around me. "Nobody is blaming you, Chloe. Filip knows you risked a lot to help him. And as sad as he is about missing En-Gin-Unity, he is still facing juvenile detention. We can still keep helping."

I'll be honest, I wasn't sure how much helping I had left in me. I thought again about how Maya was right. I wasn't a real detective. I was in over my head.

"Where's Elsie?" I asked, changing the subject.

"She's been hiding in her room this whole time," Tasha answered. "Maya is up there, too."

I told Tasha about Andrew saving me and what he had said about talking to Maya and Elsie again.

"Do you think he saw what happened?" Tasha asked.

"It sure sounded that way," I responded.

My parents finished talking to Detective Clauge and were ready to take me home. Nothing sounded more wonderful than my own bed, but I asked if I could first go upstairs and say hi to Maya and Elsie. My parents agreed, and Tasha and I made our way to Elsie's bedroom.

We opened the door without knocking. Elsie and Maya were sitting on the floor and didn't appear surprised to see us. They both looked absolutely exhausted. "Hi, Chloe," Maya said. "I'm glad you're okay." She didn't get up or offer much emotion. She handed me a notebook. "Here—I thought you might want these."

I took the notebook and looked inside. "English notes?" I asked.

"Yeah. We have a test coming up and you missed notes while you were...." She left her sentence unfinished as if she didn't want to say I was lost in the forest. "I thought they might help you."

"Thanks," I said. Something wasn't right. Maya and I were never more than distant friends. Last week she was so mad at me she had been downright rude. Why the sudden thoughtfulness? Something was definitely wrong.

I looked at Elsie, but she wouldn't look at me. "What did you tell your dad?" I asked. "I don't believe he would have gone along with leaving me out in the forest."

"It's complicated," she said.

"Obviously," I answered. I was suddenly extremely angry with Elsie. She abandoned me in the forest. I was wrong to go into the forest alone, but she left me to face one of the most frightening and dangerous experiences of my life. I could have been hurt...or worse. "What exactly did you tell your dad to get him to leave me in the forest?" I asked, my anger evident.

"I told him you were meeting a class in the forest for extra credit. I told him you were late, and the rest of the class was already in the forest and you wanted to walk with us."

"I didn't exactly walk with you," I said. "Didn't he think it was weird that I was so far behind?"

Elsie looked at Maya.

"Well?" I pressed.

"I told my dad you wanted to walk alone to go over some notes for the class."

"So when I disappeared...."

"He thought you were with the class," she finished.

"Does he know the truth?"

"He knows you weren't meeting a class. The police checked with the school after my dad told them his story."

"So did you tell him that it was your idea to ditch me in the forest?"

Elsie shook her head. "My dad thinks you are the one who lied to me and came up with the story."

This was outrageous. "So your dad thinks I'm a liar?"

"I'll fix it," she said desperately. "Just don't say anything to my dad."

I ignored her plea. "How about my parents?" I asked. "Do they think I lied to you too? Do they think I made up some crazy story about meeting a class in the woods?"

Elsie nodded.

"You had no right to do that to me," I said.

"Please," she begged. "It's complicated. You don't have all the details. You would have done the same thing."

"Why don't you give me the details and let me decide that?" I said.

Before she could answer, my dad called up the stairs and said they were ready to go. I told him I was coming.

"Please," Elsie begged one more time. "It wouldn't be so hard not to say anything. Your parents aren't going to be mad at you. They're just happy you're okay. And everyone just thinks you made up an excuse to go search for evidence. They probably think you're brave. Please, Chloe."

I didn't say anything. I turned and left with Tasha right behind me.

We walked into the kitchen and found my parents talking to Mr. and Mrs. Gowler, so we politely excused ourselves and told them we'd wait for them on the porch.

We sat on a swing together. After experiencing such deep loneliness nothing felt better than sitting next to my very best friend.

"What's going on with Elsie and Maya?" I asked.

"I don't have a clue," she answered.

"You were right," I said. "I shouldn't have gone in the forest without you. You never would have let us get lost."

"Maybe," she said. "But, Chloe, you've got guts. I've always admired that about you."

"Brains and guts," I said. "We should get t-shirts made."

"We make a great team," Tasha laughed.

Before I could agree, I saw it. At first it didn't totally register, it was more like a feeling or a connection I couldn't quite finish.

"Chloe?" Tasha asked.

I didn't answer, it was right there in front of me. I knew it, but I couldn't quite connect it.

"Chloe?"

Nothing.

"Chloe?"

I smiled. I had it.

I held up the notebook with Maya's name on it. "Look," I said.

"Maya's notes," she said. "What are you getting at?"

"Look at the name," I said.

"Maya Allsburg," Tasha read. She looked at me blankly and then back to the notebook. Suddenly she got it. "Oh," she said in a long drawn out voice. "Oh, Chloe. No way."

Sixteen

THE CASE IS CRACKED

My parents and I stayed up late into the night. I showed them what Tasha and I had discovered. I told them about Elsie's lie and got their advice on what we should do next. Then I collapsed in my warm, soft, and safe bed. Even though I only had a few hours to sleep before school, they were the most comfortable hours of my life. Spending the night in the forest had made me realize how luxurious a bed really is.

After school Tasha and I spent about twenty minutes going over our tactics that would end the biggest case of our lives.

Maya looked worried when she opened her door and found us standing on the other side. But she quickly covered by saying, "Tasha, Chloe, what a surprise. How are you feeling, Chloe?"

"Much better, thank you," I replied. "Can we chat for a few minutes?"

Maya shifted her weight. "Well, now's not a really great time. I'm supposed to be helping my mom."

"It won't take long," I said. "How about if we sit right here on your porch?"

"I'd like to, but...."

"Maya," said Tasha. "How about if I talk to your mom for you and see if she can give us a few minutes? I can even invite her out to chat with us."

If Maya looked worried when we first opened the door, now she looked downright panicked. "I'm sure it's okay for a minute," she said. She closed her front door behind her and came out to the porch.

"Have a seat." I motioned to her porch swing. I sat on one side of her and Tasha sat on the other.

"What is this about?" asked Maya.

"I think you know," said Tasha.

"I don't know what you mean," answered Maya.

"Why don't you tell us what happened that night at Elsie's?" Tasha asked.

"You know what happened," she said.

"Tell us again," I said.

Maya sighed. I'm sure she felt trapped. I'm sure she had no doubt that Tasha would go inside and get her mom. We had caught her by surprise. She was going to have to be very careful not to reveal the wrong thing.

"I was at Elsie's," she began. "We heard something. I looked out and saw Filip, and then the car was vandalized."

"What did Filip do to the car?" I asked.

"You know what he did," said Maya.

"Tell us again," Tasha said.

She sighed but continued. "He smashed it up and spray painted it."

"What did he spray paint?" I asked.

"Messages," she answered with frustration. "Messages. He spray painted messages. Can I go now?"

"What did the messages say?" asked Tasha.

I noticed sweat on Maya's upper lip. It was a cool day. "They said, *Leave or else* and *TWG*."

"What does *TWG* mean?" I asked.

"I have no idea," answered Maya.

"You have no idea?" asked Tasha. "You sure?"

"None." She was angry now.

I pulled papers out of my backpack and handed them to Maya. "You're lying," I said.

Maya paged through the papers. The first page was a

copy of the 1952 black and white photo that showed the protestor being arrested. The sign, *Leave or else,* was at his feet. The second page contained a copy of a photo that Tasha had found in the archives. It showed the second protestor arrested that day in 1952. This photo showed a second sign. It read, *Support TWG.* The next five pages contained a copy of an article that appeared in 2012 in the *Tenebray Standard*, our local paper. The article was part of a series written in honor of the sixtieth anniversary of the Tenebray Forest. This particular article contained information about the protests against the Tenebray homeowners. At the end of the article was a short bio of the author. I had highlighted it.

"Read the highlighted part," I said.

Maya was close to tears now. But she read, "Joshua Allsburg is the director of the Tenebray Historical Society. He wishes to extend a special thanks to his daughter, Maya, for working as his research assistant on this article."

"I'll ask again," said Tasha. "What does *TWG* stand for?"

Maya started to cry. "Tenebray Wildlife Group," she answered.

I pulled out a tissue from my backpack and handed it to Maya. "I think you have some explaining to do."

Seventeen

....

I UNDERSTAND WHY

When Filip called and said he was back at the police station, Tasha and I got there as quickly as possible. We arrived just in time to see Detective Clauge hand a piece of paper to Filip. "This is a copy of the official form stating all charges have been dropped."

Filip took the form, but he didn't say anything.

Detective Clauge shook both my hand and Tasha's. "You were smart to hire these two," he said to Filip.

"I know," Filip replied. He looked through the glass to where Maya and Elsie sat with their parents. "I know how it feels to be in there."

"What will happen to them?" Tasha asked.

"They have a lot of explaining to do, and I'm sure charges will be filed against them. They caused quite a mess."

Filip kept his gaze on the two girls—the two girls who had cost him En-Gin-Unity, the two girls who had been willing to send him to juvenile detention, the two girls who had threatened his future. "I understand what they did," he said.

We all looked at him like he was crazy.

"Well I don't," I said. "They got you kicked out of En-Gin-Unity and they almost cost you your freedom. You were looking at juvenile detention, Filip."

"I didn't say I wasn't angry. And I didn't mean that what they did was right or okay. I said I understood why they did it. They were scared. I was scared too, and if it hadn't been for Zocha, I was willing to lie just like they did. It's amazing what you'll consider doing when you're backed into a corner."

Eighteen

MY STRAW

Zocha was waiting for us when we walked through the door. Filip handed her the piece of paper showing that the charges had been dropped. She embraced him and when she let go, her face was wet with tears. "Come," she said. "I made hot chocolate. Chloe's favorite."

We followed her into the kitchen and while she poured the chocolate and cream into mugs, I began to explain what had happened.

"It started last week when Maya was at Elsie's house," I said. They are both on the basketball team, and Elsie had offered to help Maya with her free throws. The problem was that Elsie's parents had gone out with some friends and forgotten to move the car. It was parked under the hoop, and there was no way they could play ball with the car in the way. Elsie knew she wasn't allowed to move the car, but it seemed harmless and she figured she could return the car to the original spot before her parents got home so they'd never know. Elsie backed it right into the hoop. She ended up putting a big dent in the back bumper."

Tasha picked up the story. "Elsie panicked. She knew her parents were going to be furious. So she came up with the idea to smash up the car and make it look like a crime. Elsie moved the car back to where she thought her dad had parked it, and then they used hammers and bats to smash it up. But Elsie was still panicking that it didn't look believable enough. That's when Maya remembered the article she had worked on with her dad about the TWG. They decided if they spray painted the car with threats it would look more like a crime. They had thought enough ahead to wear gloves so the paint wouldn't be on their hands."

"They needed to hide the evidence," I said. "So after they finished the job, they wrapped up the paint and gloves in a trash bag but worried that no matter where they hid it the police would find it. Elsie knew the forest really well, so she led them both out quite far to bury the evidence.

"Then they called the police and claimed to have heard something outside. When the police arrived, they started questioning the girls. First they questioned Elsie. She hadn't expected them to ask so many questions, and she got nervous and finally said to them, 'Maya saw who did it.'

"So the police moved on to Maya. They asked her question after question—what he looked like, how tall he was, where she was standing, what he was doing, had she ever seen him before. She ended up telling the police that he looked familiar. So the police got out a school yearbook and had Maya page through to see if she could identify him. By this point she was so upset and nervous all she wanted was for it all to be over. So she pointed to a picture in the yearbook, just to get the police to stop questioning her. It was Filip's picture.

"After that, everything had been set in motion. They both knew it was wrong, but they couldn't see a way out. Suddenly they weren't just facing angry parents over a dented bumper; they had lied to the police and falsely identified Filip. They were trapped in their lies."

"How about this Andrew?" asked Zocha.

"Detective Clauge went to his house to question him this morning. Apparently he saw the whole thing."

"Why didn't he come forward?" asked Filip.

"He was afraid," answered Tasha. "He knows what people say about his family. He didn't think the police would believe his word against the girls' word.

"He said if it was so easy to frame you for the vandalism, he was worried he would be framed too. So he kept his mouth shut."

"I see," said Zocha. "Lies and silence are indeed brothers. They seem innocent, but the girls' lies and Andrew's silence almost devoured Filip."

"And lies devoured Andrew," Tasha pointed out. "Think about all the mean things people have said about Andrew's family."

"You're right," I said. "I was terrified of him at first. I believed what everyone said about him being crazy."

"So you are saying if people had been nice to Andrew he would have had the guts to come forward and save me?" asked Filip.

"Maybe," said Tasha.

Zocha shrugged. "We can never know what would have been different if small things had changed, and we mustn't forget that other people's lies and silence don't excuse our own behavior. Filip, if you had lied about committing the crime, you would have been responsible for that. Your lie would not be someone else's fault. But, I think Tasha is right. Lies and silence continue on and on and hurt more people than we realize."

"It's not just the bad stuff that goes on though," I said. I told Zocha about how carrying that boy out of the grass had inspired me. "It's weird," I told her. "You carried him out like seventy years ago, but the story of you doing it was like...." I couldn't find the right words to explain what I meant. I wanted her to know how much she meant to me and how it was her story that kept me going. And then it hit me. *Would I know where I'd fall, I'd lay some straw there ahead of time.* "You're my straw, Zocha," I said. "I had no idea I was going to fall in a forest, but when I did, your story was already there to soften what I was going through."

"You all are my straw," said Filip. "I certainly never dreamed I'd fall into criminal charges and juvenile detention, but when I did, you all softened it for me, too."

We gathered on the sofa, once again like birds in a nest. We sipped our warm hot chocolate. Zocha reached over and held my hand. I gave her hand a gentle squeeze. It seemed impossible that I had only known this great woman for a week. In that one week her story had wrapped around my own story. Her moment with that boy had become part of my moment in the forest. We may never be able to find the beginning or end of really big moments, but Zocha had taught me that our lives and the things we do stretch farther and are much greater than we will ever know.

Nineteen

THE AGENT

The following Saturday, Tasha and I planned a relaxing weekend. I slept in, and then I walked to her house for lunch. After lunch she and I made our famous triple chocolate cookies. And, because you can never have too much chocolate, I made some of Zocha's hot chocolate to wash the cookies down. We carried a tray of cookies and hot chocolate to our office where we planned on spending the afternoon doing absolutely nothing.

But life doesn't always turn out like you plan it.

Someone had stuffed an envelope under the door. I set

down the tray and picked it up. The front of the envelope had cut and pasted letters from a magazine to spell out,

Open Now.

Tasha and I exchanged worried glances, and I carefully opened the envelope and pulled out a letter. As I opened it, paper, cut into triangles, stars, and squares, fell to my feet like confetti. Tasha bent to pick them up as I looked at the letter. It was written in the same cut and pasted letters as the envelope.

I read it out loud to Tasha.

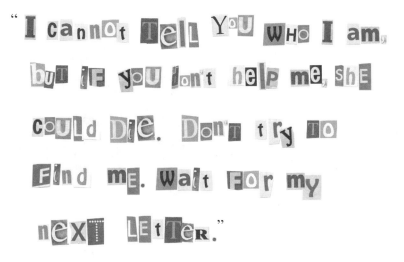

"I cannot tell you who I am, but if you don't help me, she could die. Don't try to find me. Wait for my next letter."

It was signed,

—The Agent.

A week after Tasha and Chloe solved the case, their history teacher, Ms. White, gave an assignment to write about how history impacts us today. This is Chloe's paper.

How Could it Happen?

Understanding World War II
and the Holocaust

Great Paper!

(A)

Chloe Patterson

Ms. White

World History

Chloe Patterson

Ms. White

World History

I'll be honest, I never gave much thought to World War II. It just seemed like something that happened a long time ago and didn't really mean anything to me. But then I met my friend, Zocha. She lived in Poland during World War II and helped me see that even though World War II happened before I was born, it actually did have something to do with my life. In fact, World War II showed me how hatred can spread like a disease and what happens when nobody speaks up against bad things.

Germany in Trouble

World War II took place between 1939—1945. However, in order to really understand the war you have to back up and look at how things were before the war. I'll start in the 1920's.

The Country of Germany had a lot of problems during the 1920's and early 1930's. The country was trying to recover from another massive war called World War I. When

World War I ended, people called it "The War to End All Wars." I guess people hoped that another big war would never happen. <u>Man, were they wrong or what?</u> Anyway, after World War I, Germany had a lot of debt. Germany had also lost land in the war, there weren't many jobs, and people were poor and hungry.

Don't forget to use formal language in your papers.

Bad Hope

During this time a man named Adolf Hitler started speaking to the German people. He was a passionate speaker and he could get people to pay attention to him. He promised the German people jobs, food, and more land. He told the people that Germany would be great again. Hitler promised hope. It must have felt good for the German people to have hope again. *Again, use formal language!*

The problem was that the hope that Hitler offered wasn't really hope at all. <u>I mean</u>, in my opinion, being great has a lot to do with compassion and kindness and helping others. Hitler didn't do that. Instead, he began to convince the German people they were better than other people. He told them they were a superior race. He taught that being great meant being cruel and hurting other people.

Hitler really hated Jewish people. He believed that Jews were responsible for Germany's problems—that it was their fault there wasn't enough jobs, food, and land. This wasn't true, but a lot of people started to believe it.

Legal Racism

In 1933 Hitler was ~~elected~~ *appointed. He was not actually elected.* Chancelor (the head of government) of Germany. He quickly replaced the country's democracy with his Nazi dictatorship by killing or imprisoning people who didn't agree with him. That should have been a clue that there was something wrong with the hope he was offering the German people.

Hitler turned Germany into a racist state. That meant he made it legal for people to discriminate against Jewish people. He made specific laws for Jewish people that made it illegal for them to work certain jobs. Books by Jewish authors were burned.

Hitler wanted young Germans to share his beliefs. He created the Hitler Youth Organization to teach German children to hate Jews and to love Hitler. Children were even taught to become informants—to tell the Nazis if their parents didn't support Hitler! I can't imagine ever doing something that awful to my parents.

Germany Builds an Army

After Hitler was elected, Germany started doing all sorts of things they weren't supposed to do. After World War I Germany signed something called the Treaty of Versailles that said they would not build an army. Hitler quickly broke this treaty and began building a massive army. Even though Germany broke this treaty, no countries tried to stop him. It makes me wonder what the treaty was for in the first place if nobody cared if he broke it.

Since nobody stopped him from building an army, Hitler kept on breaking more of the Treaty of Versailles. In 1936, Hitler's army moved into an area known as the Rhineland. This was German land that bordered France. For the protection of France, the Treaty of Versailles said that Germany could not put soldiers on this land. But France didn't do anything when Hitler moved troops there. I mean, again, why even *have* a treaty, right? In 1938 _—reword_ Hitler's army invaded the country of Austria. The world finally started to pay attention, but they still didn't do much. Key countries like Britain, France, the United States, and Canada didn't want to go to war. Instead of declaring war, Britain made an agreement with Hitler. They said he could have the country of Czechoslovakia as long as he promised not to invade any more countries.

Appeasing a Monster

The world thought if they gave Hitler something he wanted, he would stop invading countries. This is known as appeasement. But Hitler was not satisfied, and he did not keep his promise. Which, I mean, isn't that surprising, right? — *reword* When the kids I babysit do something wrong or throw a tantrum about something, I don't let them just have what they want. I mean, everyone knows that just sets you up for another temper tantrum five minutes later. Sometimes you have to put a screaming toddler in a chair and say, "enough" to end the whole mess. Maybe the war wouldn't have gotten so horrible if those key countries had just said, "enough" right away.

—Formal language please.

The Polish Invasion

But nobody said, "Enough!" so in 1939 Hitler invaded Poland. The Polish army tried to fight back, but they were fighting with horses and were no match for the tanks and military power of Germany. Hitler overtook Poland in only four weeks.

My friend Zocha said that Poland was a terrifying place then. Many Poles were murdered, starved, or used as slaves. The Polish Jews were the worst off. The Polish Jews were forced to live together in ghettos. They had to wear a Star of David so they could be recognized as a Jew. By 1942, Hitler set out to kill every single Polish Jew—every man, woman, and child. The Jews were sent to horrible camps to be murdered. These camps were called concentration camps.

War is Declared

After the invasion of Poland, the countries of Britain and France finally declared war on Germany. A few days later, Canada declared war as well. However, the countries did very little to stop Hitler from continuing to conquer nations across Europe. Hitler did have a few allies. Allies are countries that join together for military action. Japan and Italy sided with Germany. Even though countries had declared war on Germany, by 1940 Hitler had invaded most of Europe without anyone trying to stop him. Crazy.

The United States is Attacked

On December 7, 1941, Japan, one of Germany's allies, attacked Pearl Harbor, Hawaii. The United States declared war and joined in fighting against Germany and its allies. The countries who had united against Hitler were known as the Allied Forces.

The Fall of Germany

World War II lasted for three and a half more years. In the spring of 1945, Germany was no longer able to hold off the Allied Forces. A few days before losing the war, Hitler killed himself. He left behind a letter expressing his pride in his killing of Jewish people. That makes me sick.

—It makes me sick too.

Shortly after his death, Soviet soldiers (part of the Allied Forces) marched into Berlin, Germany. Germany formally surrendered, or gave up, on May 7, 1945.

The Atom Bombs *should be "Atomic"*

During the summer of 1945, the Japanese continued to fight. They refused to surrender. The United States was eager for the war to be over so they decided to use a powerful new weapon against Japan—the atom bomb.

atomic

The Allied Forces gave Japan one last warning but they refused to surrender.

On August 6, 1945, the United States dropped an atomic bomb on Hiroshima, Japan. On August 9, 1945, a second bomb was dropped on Nagasaki, Japan. The *atomic* ~~atom~~ bomb was the most horrific weapon ever used. The heat and light from the blast instantly killed thousands of people. The initial blast was followed by a firestorm. Because the *atomic* ~~atom~~ bomb contains nuclear radiation, many people later became ill and died. In Hiroshima, it is estimated that between 80,000 and 140,000 people died as a result of the *atomic* ~~atom~~ bomb. In Nagasaki, it is estimated that between 35,000 and 70,000 died. Like I said, it was a horrible weapon. A lot of the people who were hurt and died were just plain old citizens.

—instead use, "civilians"

The Aftermath

Japan formally surrendered on September 2, 1945 and the war ended. However, even after the war ended, people's lives were still in ruins. No one knows exactly how many people were killed, but it is estimated that about 20 million soldiers died in the war and between 30 and 35 million civilians were killed. More than 20 million homes were destroyed. Entire communities were in ruins with schools, businesses, and factories all destroyed.

The Holocaust

I've talked about how the war started and ended, but you really can't talk about World War II without talking about the Holocaust. The Holocaust was Nazi Germany's plan to persecute and kill Jews living in Europe. The Nazis also targeted Gypsies, the handicapped, and Poles (people from Poland).

Why did Hitler want the Jews to die? He argued that Jews were evil and responsible for all of Germany's problems. He believed that Jews were less than human and filthy and that the world would be better off if they didn't exist. Hitler's final solution to his problem with Jews was to kill every man, woman, and child who was Jewish. It is important to know that the Jewish people did nothing to deserve this. They are not to blame for what was done to them.

Not all German people believed that Jews were bad. In fact, many non-Jewish Germans shopped at Jewish stores and were neighbors and friends with Jewish people. Hitler knew that he had to convince the German population to hate Jews. He began by terrorizing, beating, and killing people who opposed him and his ideas. Hitler's brutal police force encouraged people to commit violence against Jewish people. They also encouraged Germans to damage Jewish property. Acts of violence against Jews were encouraged and never punished. I can't even imagine living somewhere where the police want you to hurt other people. That makes me feel really great about living in a country where the police help.

Hitler controlled newspapers and other publications. He had articles written for these publications to explain how Jews had hurt Germany. Slowly, Hitler's beliefs started to become accepted in Germany. Many people started to believe that Hitler was right and the Jews needed to be wiped out. Most people who disagreed with Hitler remained silent. That's the part that bothers me. I mean, it seems like the whole mess got as big as it did because nobody wanted to say anything. The countries around her didn't want to tell Germany to stop and the people didn't want to speak up either. I know it's easy to think I would have done something differently. It was a very scary time. But I guess I hope I would have had the guts to speak up. Anyway, Hitler had succeeded in convincing a large part of a nation that all Jews, even children, deserved to die.

Most Jews were killed in concentration camps. These camps were set up to efficiently murder as many Jews as possible. As Hitler invaded countries across Europe, Jews were taken by cattle cars to these concentration camps. The Nazis sometimes used the people in these brutal prison camps for slave labor; however, people were also starved, tortured, and murdered. I'm pretty good with words, but I've been sitting here completely blank on how to describe the horrible system of death Hitler created. It is just too awful for words to even describe. _I agree._

Some non-Jewish people helped hide their Jewish neighbors and friends. This was a very risky thing to do. If these non-Jewish people were caught, they too were sent to a concentration camp or killed.

In 1945, when Hitler was defeated, the Allied soldiers (soldiers from countries who fought against Hitler) liberated the concentration camps—they rescued people who were still there. Many who survived the concentration camps returned home to find that their entire family had been murdered. By the time the war ended the Nazi's had murdered six million Jews. In some countries, like Poland, ninety percent of all Jewish people were killed. In all, Hitler had succeeded in wiping out about two-thirds of Europe's Jews.

How Could this happen?

My friend Zocha was one of the people during the war who didn't just stay silent. She risked her life to rescue a little boy. *Her example* ~~She~~ helped me see that in a lot of ways what happened during the war really keeps happening over and *Excellent point!* over again. I mean, maybe not on such a big scale, but how many times have I looked the other way or stayed silent because getting involved was risky? And the thing is, it isn't even half as risky as what Zocha did. In my life, "risky" pretty much means losing popularity at school. While I was researching the war I told myself that if I lived during World War II, I'd be some hero who spoke up. But the truth is that if I don't have the guts to speak up even at school or around friends, who am I to say I would have been brave like my friend, Zocha? When I started thinking about that, I knew I had to change the way I made decisions.

> The Holocaust was not an accident in history—it occurred because individuals, organizations, and governments made choices that not only legal-ized discrimination but also allowed prejudice, hatred, and ultimately mass murder to occur.
>
> -The United States Holocaust Museum

Choices are important when it comes to the Holocaust. There were a lot of people who chose to do really horrible things. But there were also a lot of people who chose to do nothing. Until I met my friend Zocha, I had never really thought about silence as a choice. Silence just seemed, well, like nothing. But now I see how being silent is really an action and it can have really bad consequences.

Great points here!

> The Holocaust provides a context [or a way] for exploring the dangers of remaining silent, apathetic, and indifferent in the face of the oppression of others.
>
> -The United States Holocaust Museum

In closing, I don't think it is enough to simply learn about the horrors of the Holocaust. We also have to ask and understand how something so horrible could happen. We have to recognize the dangerous power of doing nothing. We need to learn that looking the other way is an action that can lead to really horrible things. And then, once we learn this, we need to find the courage to live it like my friend Zocha did. We need to find the courage to no longer stay silent in the face of injustice.

Great ending!

Glossary

Allied Forces – The countries that joined together to fight against Germany, Japan, and Italy.

Appeasement – The policy used by the British to give Hitler what he wanted in exchange for peace.

Democracy – A political system that is governed by elected officials.

Ghettos – Sections of a city where Jewish people were forced to live.

The Holocaust – The mass murder of Jews under Nazi Germany rule. Six million Jews were murdered. The Holocaust also targeted Gypsies, the handicapped, and Poles (people from Poland).

Nazi Party – A racist, authoritarian government (a government who forces obedience) who ruled Germany between 1933 and 1945.

Racist State – A country with racist and harmful laws directed at a certain race of people.

Surrender – To give up fighting and submit to another nation.

Treaty of Versailles – The peace treaty that ended World War I. Many Germans felt that this treaty was very unfair toward them.